D0115612

Missy
Piggle-Wiggle
and the
Whatever
Cure

Based on the Mrs. Piggle-Wiggle series of
books and characters created by Betty MacDonald
and Anne MacDonald Canham

Missy Piggle-Wiggle

and the

Whatever Cure

ANN M. MARTIN

with ANNIE PARNELL

illustrated by BEN HATKE

SQUARE
FISH

Feiwel and Friends
New York

SQUARE
FISH

An imprint of Macmillan Publishing Group, LLC
175 Fifth Avenue, New York, NY 10010
mackids.com

MISSY PIGGLE-WIGGLE AND THE WHATEVER CURE.
Text copyright © 2016 by Ann M. Martin, Inc. and Elliam Corp.
Illustrations copyright © 2016 by Ben Hatke. All rights reserved.
Rights in the original characters created by Betty MacDonald and
Anne MacDonald Canham are reserved to the creators.
All rights reserved. Printed in the United States of America by LSC
Communications, Harrisonburg, Virginia

Square Fish and the Square Fish logo are trademarks of Macmillan and
are used by Feiwel and Friends under license from Macmillan.

Our books may be purchased in bulk for promotional, educational, or business use.
Please contact your local bookseller or the Macmillan Corporate and Premium
Sales Department at (800) 221-7945 ext. 5442 or by e-mail at
MacmillanSpecialMarkets@macmillan.com.

Library of Congress Cataloging-in-Publication Data

Names: Martin, Ann M., 1955– author. | Parnell, Annie, author.
Title: Missy Piggle-Wiggle and the Whatever Cure / Ann M. Martin with Annie
Parnell.
New York : Feiwel & Friends, 2016. | Summary: "Mrs. Piggle-Wiggle has left her
Upside-Down House and the animals that live there in the care of her twenty-
something niece, Missy. Luckily for the town's families, Missy Piggle-Wiggle
is capable of concocting the same sort of inventive cures for bad behavior that
made her aunt an indispensable community resource"—Provided by publisher.
Identifiers: LCCN 2015036613 | ISBN 978-1-250-12953-6 (paperback) |
ISBN 978-1-250-10019-1 (ebook)
Subjects: | CYAC: Behavior—Fiction. | Humorous stories. | BISAC: JUVENILE
FICTION / Fantasy & Magic.
Classification: LCC PZ7.M3567585 Ml 2016 | DDC [Fic]—dc23
LC record available at https://lccn.loc.gov/2015036613

Originally published in the United States by Feiwel and Friends
First Square Fish edition, 2017
Book designed by Eileen Savage
Square Fish logo designed by Filomena Tuosto

10 9 8 7 6 5 4 3 2 1

AR: 4.9 / LEXILE: 720L

For Betty MacDonald, and the magic she brought
to my childhood and to generations of readers
—A. M. M.

~~~~~~~

For Will and Elsie, who taught me that we all need
a cure every now and then, even though we're perfect
—A. P.

Contents

Missy Piggle-Wiggle

and the

Whatever Cure

Dear Missy,

As you know, my husband, Mr. Piggle-Wiggle, was called away some years ago by the pirates. After waiting so long for him to return, I have decided to take matters into my own hands and find out what happened to him. I'll be leaving tomorrow. While I'm gone, could you stay at the farm and live in the upside-down house? I'm sorry to ask you to leave your home and your work, but I need you. Harold Spectacle will take care of the animals until you arrive in Little Spring Valley.

I'm sure you remember what to do for Wag, Lightfoot, Lester, and the others. Everything at the upside-down house is just as it was the last time you were here.

I apologize for the haste with which I'm making these preparations. Some things can't be helped.

Please come as quickly as you can.

Sending you love,
Auntie

1

Missy Piggle-Wiggle

THE MOST WONDERFUL thing about the town of Little Spring Valley was not its magic shop, and not the fact that one day a hot-air balloon had appeared as if from nowhere and floated over the town and no one ever knew where it had come from, and not even the fact that the children could play outside and run all up and down the streets willy-nilly without their parents hovering over them. No, the most wonderful thing about the town was the upside-down house, and of course the little woman who lived in it.

The upside-down house had been built for Missy's great-aunt, Mrs. Piggle-Wiggle, by her husband,

Mr. Piggle-Wiggle the pirate. It was the house Mrs. Piggle-Wiggle had dreamed of when she was a little girl, with ceilings for floors and floors for ceilings and light fixtures growing up beneath your feet that must be stepped around as you tromp through the house. Missy had looked forward to her childhood visits to the upside-down house and the little lady who was known for her great understanding of children. She had been allowed to visit without her mother, who had no patience for a house standing on its head, not to mention her aunt's fondness for magic. Mrs. Piggle-Wiggle, whom Missy called Auntie, had thought up playing Cinderella as a way of getting the beds made, and garbage races as a way of taking the trash cans to the street on garbage-collection day, and pirate parties as a way to clean house, with a great deal of heave-ho-ing and the tossing out of dirty dishwater accompanied by a cry of "Man overboard!"

Since Mrs. Piggle-Wiggle was indeed magic, she kept a cupboard stocked with potions and powders and vapory things meant to cure children of any number of bad habits. Missy's mother was disdainful of these cures, which is a polite way of saying that she mocked and scorned them. The grown-ups in Little Spring Valley, however, were very grateful to Mrs. Piggle-Wiggle for her help with their children's selfishness and tiny-bite eating and bath avoidance.

Living with Mrs. Piggle-Wiggle were Wag the dog, Lightfoot the cat, Penelope the talking parrot, and Lester the pig, who didn't talk but who had exquisite manners and also liked to drink four or five cups of coffee at every meal. The yard around the upside-down house was where Mr. Piggle-Wiggle had buried his pirate treasure, and when Missy was a little girl and not busy practicing magic of her own, she had spent many hours digging for gold. The children of the town did the same thing now, so the yard was always full of holes, which Mrs. Piggle-Wiggle didn't care about one bit as long as the children eventually planted flowers in the holes.

Missy Piggle-Wiggle arrived in Little Spring Valley on a warm morning exactly three days after she had received the letter from her great-aunt, and exactly two days after she had reluctantly left her new post at the Magic Institute for Children. She'd stuck the letter in the band of her straw hat, and now she plucked it out and read it again as she approached the upside-down house. The letter had been written in haste, and she wondered why. She also wondered why Mrs. Piggle-Wiggle had suddenly decided to search for her husband. Where did one look for pirates, anyway? Furthermore, who was Harold Spectacle?

The sun shone on Missy as she returned the letter to her hat and made her way down the street again. A hummingbird buzzed by on its way to a pot of petunias. On the front porch of a tidy yellow house, a sleeping cat woke up suddenly, leaped at a fly, and went back to its bed. Missy switched her suitcase from one hand to the other. She shaded her eyes and said aloud, "Ah. There it is."

Ahead of her was a small brown house with its bottom sticking up into the sky and the roof poking into the ground. Missy was at once confronted by two feelings that seemed to have very little to do with each other. She felt happy longing for the childhood days she had spent with Auntie, learning about the potions and practicing her own magic (she was a quick learner, not afraid to make mistakes, no matter how many things accidentally levitated or disappeared), and she felt an anxious prickling around her ears and behind her eyes as she recalled that the upside-down house could sometimes behave like a rude and obstinate child. It loved Mrs. Piggle-Wiggle. It also had an excellent memory for Missy's childhood mishaps and had never recovered from the unfortunate afternoon when she had unintentionally converted the upside-down house to a right-side-up house. Missy had reversed the magic in a matter of seconds, but the house didn't forgive her until she had apologized 671 times.

Missy hesitated at the end of the walk that led to the front door. The door was located in the peak formed by the roof. There were two knobs on it, one high up where you'd find a knob if you turned a door upside down and a reachable one closer to the ground.

"I'm coming, House," she whispered. She shaded her eyes and thought she could see figures in the windows. Lester's snout and Penelope's beak, Wag and Lightfoot standing on their hind legs with their paws against the panes of glass. Missy set one foot on the path.

The stone tilted to the left, and Missy clutched at her suitcase. "I'm still coming," she called. "Can't you forgive me, House? I'm really sorry. There. That's my six hundred and seventy-second apology."

The second stone sank into the ground as if Missy had stepped on a lily pad in a pond. She let out a sigh but bravely heaved herself out of the hole and marched toward the door, wobbling and weaving as the path shifted beneath her.

When she reached the front steps, she dropped her suitcase smartly on the wooden boards. "Auntie asked me to come here," she told the house. "She needs my help and . . . that's that!"

The envelope enclosing the letter to Missy from her great-aunt had also held a key to the house. Missy now withdrew the key from her purse. She stuck it in the lower doorknob. The knob let out a scream, and Missy drew the key back with a smile. "Very funny, House," she said. "You know you're going to have to let me in sooner or later."

She inserted the key in the lock a second time and heard nothing. She turned the key. The knob disappeared.

"Don't you dare!" exclaimed Missy. She waited

twenty seconds for the knob to reappear (which is a long time if you're doing nothing but standing and staring and waiting). "All right," said Missy at last. "Two can play at this game." She flicked her hand, the door hinges unfastened themselves, the door fell forward into the hallway, and Missy plucked up her suitcase and stepped inside.

Slowly the knob reappeared, the key still in the lock.

"Thank you," said Missy. She flicked her wrist again. The door bumped itself upright, and the pins slid back into the hinges. "I certainly hope we're not going to have to go through that every time I want to get inside."

She heard faint laughter from the walls of the house.

In the dim light, Missy could now see Wag, Lightfoot, Penelope, and Lester standing in a row in the foyer. Wag was wagging his tail, which, of course, was why he had been named Wag in the first place, and his mouth was hanging open, which might have been because of the crashing door or might simply have been because he was a dog. Lightfoot was standing with her back to Missy, her tail twitching dangerously.

Penelope was staring, unblinking, her head cocked to one side. Lester attempted to recover from his surprise. He put a smile on his face and stuck out his right front hoof. Missy shook it.

"Lightfoot," said Missy, "is something wrong? Did I scare you? I'm sorry if I did."

The cat threw a reproachful glance over her shoulder and slunk away.

"A bad time is what it is," squawked Penelope. "A bad time. A bad time."

Missy turned to Wag and put her arms around his neck. "I'm glad to see you," she murmured.

Wag wagged his tail again and licked her ear.

"Well," said Missy smartly as she straightened up. "There's nothing to do but get right to work and set things in order. Let's get organized."

"Time to feed us. That's what Mrs. Piggle-Wiggle would do," said Penelope, flapping her wings. "Feed us."

"It isn't your dinnertime and you know it," said Missy.

"Mrs. Piggle-Wiggle would give us a snack."

"Would she? Well, we'll see. Now. I know Auntie

must have left me—ah, here it is." Missy caught sight of an envelope on a table by the doorway. She reached for it, and the envelope was whisked into the air. "House! Return that, please!"

The envelope floated to the floor. Missy picked it up, slit it open, and drew out a single sheet of paper. She stepped over a doorway and carried the paper into the parlor, where she sat on a great fluffy chair next to a dollhouse that one of Mrs. Piggle-Wiggle's many child visitors had been building out of Popsicle sticks, paper-towel tubes, and feathers.

Missy read the note aloud to Lester, who had followed her into the parlor and seated himself on a sofa with his hind legs crossed just so. She read slowly because the hastily written note was nearly impossible to decipher.

Dear Missy,

If you are reading this, then you have found your way to Little Spring Valley and the upside-down house. Thank you for coming.

The food for Wag, Lightfoot, and Penelope

is in the kitchen cupboard next to the stove.
You will know which is for whom because the
containers are labeled. Lester eats human
food from the refrigerator and will sit at the
table with you because of his extreme good
manners.

Here Missy glanced at Lester, who nodded and
smiled at her, and then blushed slightly. Missy patted
his hoof and returned to the letter.

The food for the barn animals is in the barn.
Feeding instructions are tacked up on the wall
by Trotsky's stall.
I asked Harold Spectacle, who owns A to Z
Books, the bookstore on Juniper Street, to come
by twice a day to feed the animals. Please let
him know when you arrive and thank him for
helping out.

Sending love,
Auntie

PS There's a family—

Here Missy slowed down and stopped reading altogether. "Auntie has the most atrocious handwriting," she remarked to Lester.

Lester nodded sympathetically.

"What's this word?" she asked, and held the note in front of him. "Can you read it?"

Lester frowned. He took the paper in his hooves and turned it around and around and around. Then he shrugged and handed the note back.

Missy stared at the scrawled words. "A family in trouble?" she murmured. "A family named Freeforall who's having trouble with their children? I think this is their address. Do you know the Freeforalls, Lester?"

Lester nodded and looked very sad.

"Well, if there's trouble with the children, then I must visit them. Don't worry, Lester. I'm here to help. I'll get things sorted out. But first things first."

Missy picked up her suitcase. "Come with me, Wag," she said as she approached the stairs.

Wag stood up from where he'd been sleeping under a table and shook himself.

Missy set her foot on the first step and then fell forward as the staircase vanished. "House! Put it back!" she commanded as Wag licked her face with concern.

The staircase reappeared. It was six inches tall. Missy hid a smile, but Wag growled nervously and eyed the second floor.

"Full-size!" said Missy.

The staircase grew and then slid toward the parlor, bumping against the ceiling.

"Put it back as it was and where it belongs!" ordered Missy. "Right now."

The staircase returned to the center of the foyer. Wag looked warily at it.

"It's okay," said Missy. "House and I have known each other a long time." She carried her suitcase upstairs, Wag at her heels, turned right, and walked down the hall to the room she always stayed in when she visited.

The door was closed. "House, I hope this door is unlocked," said Missy. She reached cautiously for the knob and turned it. "Thank you," she said.

The room was as she remembered it. A bed covered with a neat white spread, a blue quilt folded across the foot. A chest of drawers, a window framed by blue-and-white-flowered curtains, and a wooden cabinet in the corner. The cabinet was painted blue. Missy tugged at the door. It was locked.

This was not the fault of the house. The door was supposed to be locked. Missy withdrew a locket and removed a small brass key with a bit of pink ribbon tied to one end. She inserted the key into the lock. The door creaked open.

"My potions," said Missy with satisfaction. "Just as I left them." She took in the rows of small bottles and jars and tins, each labeled with the name of the unwanted habit it would cure. She lifted a square purple bottle from the middle shelf. "'Won't-Take-a-Bath Cure,'" she read. She uncorked the bottle and sniffed it. "Mmm. Grapy. Remember when I tried this on you, Wag? Wag?"

Missy caught sight of Wag's tail disappearing around the corner as he crept into the hall. "I'm not going to do it again!" she called after him. "I was only little then. I was still learning the magic."

But Wag was gone. Missy made short work of arranging her clothes in the bureau drawers. She lined up her shoes in the closet and placed a stack of books by her bed. She reached into her suitcase for pajamas, her toothbrush, her slippers, and her woolen cold-weather hat. At last she pulled out the satchel that she would take with her to the Freeforalls' that afternoon.

Downstairs, Missy walked through the kitchen, where Lightfoot had jumped to the top of Mrs. Piggle-Wiggle's funny old black stove and was surveying the room.

"Come with me to the barn," Missy called to the animals as she let herself out the back door. But only Penelope followed, wings flapping as she thrust herself through the door just before it closed.

"Could have squished me!" she called. "Ever heard of holding a door open? Could have squished me."

"Sorry," said Missy. "Luckily, you're an excellent flier. Now, remind me who's out in the barn."

"Why, Trotsky the horse, of course; Heather the cow; and Pulitzer the owl. Warren the gander; Warren's wife, Evelyn Goose; Martha and Millard Mallard. And the chickens and rabbits and turkeys are around somewhere. The sheep are in the pasture."

Missy stepped through the door to the barn, which

was not upside-down but a regular barn. An upside-down house was one thing, but an upside-down barn, with the stalls in the air and the hayloft on the ground, would have caused all sorts of problems, such as how to coax a horse and cow upstairs to their beds each night, and how to pitch hay up above one's head.

Missy peered into the dim light and leaned back to look into the rafters. There perched Pulitzer, sound asleep since it was hours before his hunting time.

Missy peeked in the stalls. "Hello, Trotsky. Hello, Heather," she said. She patted their backs. Then she led them outside and turned them into the pasture with the sheep.

There were always so many farm chores to take care of, but Missy could see that Harold Spectacle had done a good job. The troughs were filled with clean water. There was fresh straw in the stalls. The rabbit hutches and turkey pens had been scrubbed.

"Harold seems very responsible," Missy remarked approvingly.

"Snack time! Snack time!" squawked Penelope.

Missy eyed the parrot. "I don't remember seeing

anything about snack time for the animals in Auntie's instructions," she replied. "But let's go back in the house and look again." She crossed the yard, pausing to admire Warren and Evelyn's goslings on the way.

Penelope flapped along, and Missy remembered to hold the back door open for her. In the kitchen, Missy looked in a cupboard and found the container of parrot food.

"I'm afraid it doesn't mention snacks here," she said, stroking Penelope's feathers. "Sometimes we wish something so hard that it begins to seem real when it's really just in our imagination."

Penelope looked away and muttered, "We want snack time," over and over until the shade above the kitchen window began to snap up and down, up and down.

Missy clapped her hands together as Penelope let out a startled squawk. "House, that's quite enough out of you. You frightened Penelope!" The house creaked and groaned. "I'm going to be here for a while," Missy continued. "So we'd better learn to get along. Now I'm off to pay a visit to Harold, and then I'll see about the Freeforalls. I wonder where Merriweather Court is."

Missy went back to her room to retrieve her satchel, the one that was always so helpful when dealing with children. She heaved it over her shoulder, and it disappeared from view. She took one last look at her cupboard of potions, and then she called for Wag.

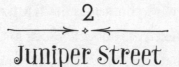

2
Juniper Street

MISSY CLIPPED WAG'S leash to his collar and patted the satchel that hung over her shoulder. She couldn't see the satchel, but it was comforting to know it was there.

"Ready for a walk, Wag?" she asked.

Wag wagged his tail, then sat on his haunches by the door.

"Good-bye, Lightfoot; good-bye, Penelope; good-bye, Lester," Missy called. "Good-bye, House." She added, "Lester, you're in charge while I'm out."

Lester straightened his back and smiled at her.

But Penelope, who was perched on the banister, rustled her feathers and hopped up and down, squawking, "A fine thing! A fine thing!"

"Please behave yourselves," said Missy. She let Wag outside and locked the door. The lock got a firm grip on her key and held tight. Missy stepped back and looked at the house. It was the same look she would give a child who has asked for an ice-cream cone forty-five times in one afternoon. The same look she would give a brother and sister who are holding on to a basketball and pulling it back and forth yelling, "It's my turn!" "No, it's my turn!" "No, it's *my* turn!" "No, it's MY turn!" The same look she once gave a little boy who had interrupted her while she was on the phone in order to whisper urgently, "At snack time, give me the biggest cookie."

"*House*," said Missy warningly. She heard a faint rattling from the doorknob as the house released the key. Missy relaxed. "Thank you."

Missy and Wag made it safely along the path to the sidewalk. The stones shifted only once. The moment they did, Missy gave the house another look, and the stones settled down and behaved themselves.

Missy turned onto the street. Wag trotted ahead of

her, tail held high like a flag. He paused often to sniff the air, then trotted on again once he had given his approval of whatever scent had attracted his attention.

Missy looked at the familiar sights of Little Spring Valley. It was a quiet Saturday morning. Children rode their bicycles and played tag and climbed trees and called to one another. On one porch an old man and an old woman sat side by side, holding hands.

Missy had just caught sight of Juniper Street, the street where all the stores and interesting things were, when she spotted a girl in front of a large house painted blue with yellow shutters and a pink porch. The girl was standing at a gate at the end of a walk, leaning against it in a sad sort of way, her chin resting on her crossed arms.

"Hi!" Missy called to her.

The girl shifted her eyes from the nothingness she'd been staring at to Missy and Wag. "Hi," she said forlornly.

"I'm Missy Piggle-Wiggle and this is Wag."

"I'm Melody Flowers." She swung back and forth on the gate. "I guess you're my new neighbor."

"Do you know Mrs. Piggle-Wiggle?" asked Missy.

"I met her twice, but I just moved here, and I really don't know anybody at all."

"Hasn't anyone come to call?"

"They did, but I hid in my room."

"What about friends at school?"

"I haven't made any yet."

My goodness, thought Missy. *Melody certainly is shy.* "Wag and I are walking into town," she told her. "Why don't you come with us?"

Melody continued to swing on the gate. "Are you Mrs. Piggle-Wiggle's niece?" she asked.

"I'm her great-niece."

"Are you staying in that upside-down house?"

"Yes."

"How do you sleep upside down?"

"Haven't you been in the upside-down house?" asked Missy. Almost every child in Little Spring Valley had been in the upside-down house at one time or another. They knew how things worked there.

"Nope. We only moved here two weeks and one day ago. Do you sleep upside down like a bat?"

"Heavens, no. I sleep right side up in a bed. It's just that the bed is on the floor, but the floor is the ceiling."

Missy pointed ahead of her to an intersection. "Wag and I are going to explore Juniper Street. Then we're going to see if we can find Harold Spectacle at A to Z Books."

Melody looked directly at Missy. "The bookstore?"

"Aha! You're a reader," said Missy.

"How can you tell?"

"By your eyes. True readers look fond and excited when the subject of books and bookstores comes up."

"I can take you to the bookstore," exclaimed Melody. "I know exactly where it is. I'll be right back." Melody dashed to her house, clattered up the front steps, and returned a few minutes later. "My mom says it's okay for me to go with you."

So Melody set off with Missy and Wag. She walked behind them until Missy called over her shoulder, "Wag and I are terribly lonely up here, and we'd love to have some company." Then Melody hurried ahead and walked by Missy's side. She kept glancing at Wag's leash until Missy handed it to her and said, "I only let extremely responsible people walk him."

Melody smiled.

At the intersection, Missy turned right. "Juniper Street at last," she said.

All up and down Juniper Street were the stores and businesses of Little Spring Valley. "My, it's been a long time since my last visit with Auntie," said Missy.

"Auntie?"

"Mrs. Piggle-Wiggle. I call her Auntie. I haven't been here in ages. Now, where is A to Z Books? I don't think there was a bookstore on Juniper Street the last time I visited."

"It's up there!" cried Melody. "See the sign with the open book?"

"Ah. Wonderful. Let's not go right away, though," said Missy. "Let's explore a little first. Have you ever been an explorer?"

"Well, no," said Melody, frowning.

"No matter. Have you ever been a twin?"

"Have I *ever* been a twin? That's a funny question."

"Not at all. We can pretend to be twins right now."

"But—but—"

"I know we don't look alike, but not all twins do," said Missy.

"Aren't we supposed to be the same age, though?" asked Melody.

"Don't be so serious. Come along. We're the explorer twins. And Wag is our intrepid Saint Bernard."

"He is?"

"Of course. And we've just come upon a town that sprang up before our very eyes. Oh my." Missy shaded her eyes and stared ahead.

"What? What is it?"

"Why, it's Aunt Martha's General Store. Our very first sighting of a general store! Record that in our journal, Flowers."

"Um, okay." Melody pretended to open a book and write in it. Then she said, "So I guess your last name is Flowers, too. Since we're twins."

"No, I'm still a Piggle-Wiggle. Come along, Explorer Flowers. What else do you see?"

Melody grinned. "I see . . . wait—yes, it's a coffee shop! 'Bean's Coffee Shop,'" she added, reading the sign. "'Proprietors—Dean and Jean Bean.'"

Missy peered through the window. "I believe we should buy some refreshment. We've been exploring for days. I'm parched."

Missy and Melody bought iced tea and sipped it at a table outside. Wag fell asleep under their chairs while Melody told Missy about a store called the Art of Magic on a side street. She leaned across the table and whispered, "It's spooky. I went in, and it was all dark and dusty, and there was a black cat in a basket, and the nameplate on the basket read Mephistopheles."

"No!" said Missy.

"Yes. And there was no one in the store at first, and then this man dressed all in black suddenly stepped in front of me and began speaking in the language of Magic. Really," said Melody, as if Missy had doubted her. He said, 'Deplow ees fronket phooey?' and somehow I knew that was Magic for 'How may I help you?'" Melody shivered.

"You'll have to show me the store later." Missy stood up and woke Wag.

"Are we the explorer twins again?" asked Melody.

"No, now we are French. *Ooh-la-la. Qu'est-ce que c'est?*"

"I don't exactly speak French," said Melody. "Could we be something else?"

"*Bien sûr.* What would you like to be?"

"Tourists," replied Melody. "And after that, long-lost relatives."

Melody and Missy and Wag set off again. They peeked into a grocery store and introduced themselves to Mr. Duchess, the owner. They passed the post office, where Mary Grace and her cats were at work behind the window. They passed a dental office, a hardware store, two clothing stores, a shoe store, and a sewing store.

"And across the street is the library," said Melody, pointing.

"Ah, the library. I remember it well."

What Missy actually remembered was the day when she was ten years old, still experimenting with her magic, and, in the lobby, she had opened a vial of orange vapor that she hoped would correct children who had the bad habit of not returning books on time. Missy wanted the overdue books returned so that she could read them herself. Instead, when she uncorked the bottle, she heard cries of "Oh, ew! What is that smell?" "It smells like rotten eggs!" "It smells like poop!" "Where is it coming from?" Before she knew it, the library had been evacuated, and she was the only person left in it, hiding behind a shelf of mysteries. The potion did absolutely nothing to cure the problem of overdue library books.

Of course, Missy didn't mention this to Melody. Some things were better kept to oneself.

Melody suddenly clutched at Missy's arm. "Look! Down there! It's Spell Street. That's where the Art of Magic is."

"What fun!" exclaimed Missy. "Let's be explorers again. I want to see the Art of Magic for myself."

"No!" shrieked Melody. Then she said more calmly, "I mean, no. Not today. Some other time. Let's go to A to Z Books now. Please?"

"Very well."

Like her great-aunt, Missy understood that it is better not to push certain children. "Onward to the bookstore," she said.

Melody Flowers hustled along, turning her head now and then to glance at Missy. What an odd woman Missy was, with her big straw hat and her wild red hair springing out from under it, and her shoes, which were sparkly and red. She was quite short, not much taller than Melody, who wasn't very tall for a ten-year-old, and she was as skinny as a stick. She wore a dress with a beautiful shawl, even on this warm day, and the colors of the dress reminded Melody of an ocean—green and blue and aqua. The shawl shimmered with sequins, which Missy had sewn on herself, although of course Melody didn't know this. All she knew was that here was an adult who treated her like a person, not like a child, and who understood how it felt to be afraid of magic shops and new neighbors.

Melody slipped one hand into Missy's and clutched Wag's leash with her other hand, since she wanted to continue to demonstrate how responsible she was. Together, Melody and Missy crossed the street to A to Z Books.

"Now, the first thing to know about the bookstore," said Melody as they stood outside, "is that the bell over the door sounds like a sneeze. So I guess it isn't really a bell."

"A sneeze," said Missy. "How original."

"Harold says it can get confusing if someone inside the store actually sneezes. He doesn't know whether to greet a customer or to say 'Gesundheit.' But the sneezing door is so loud that mostly he can tell the difference."

Missy reached for the door and pushed it open.

AH-AH-AH-CHOO!

"Hello?" called a voice from the back.

"Hi, Harold. It's me, Melody," said Melody. "And Missy Piggle-Wiggle."

"You'll have to speak up," Missy told her. "I don't think he can hear that soft voice."

Melody looked helplessly at Missy. "I don't like to yell."

"You don't like to yell?" Missy was more used to yelling children who needed to lower the volume on their voices. "Well, that's all right. Just speak up, then." She gave Melody's hand a squeeze.

"Hi, Harold," said Melody in a voice that was even smaller than before.

From the back of the store hurried a very tall young man who, you could tell right away, cared a great deal about his appearance. He wore a top hat with a daisy stuck in the band. Most top hats are made from black silk, but Harold's was red velvet. He wore a red velvet tuxedo, too, and the tails of the jacket were so long they reached the backs of his knees. His shoes, which were a soothing shade of purple, were highly polished. Missy saw a black cane leaning against the checkout counter, and she wondered whether Harold actually needed it or if it was for show. It would go quite nicely with his outfit.

Harold rushed toward the door so fast that Missy decided then and there that his cane must be for show. He hurtled between shelves, knocking several books to the floor in his rush.

"Oh dear! Oh my!" he exclaimed. "I've knocked *Treasure Island* down. Now, that's a book you don't want to miss reading. Have you read it yet, Melody? Oh, and there goes *Half Magic*." He scrambled to his knees, gathered up the books, returned them to their spots on the shelves, then banged into *Caps for Sale* and *Make Way for Ducklings* as he tore through the picture-book section.

"I'll get them," said Melody.

"Thank you. Thank you, Melody. By the way, a new book has come in that you must take a look at. It's up by the register." Harold rounded a corner and stopped short when he caught sight of Missy, who had stopped short at the sight of Harold and was gazing at him, her mouth open. Harold stuck his hand out toward her, tripped over a display of a book about cats that can paint, and fell against Missy's shoulder.

A shower of sparks glittered briefly in the air and sputtered out.

Missy and Harold stared at each other.

"I just," Missy began breathlessly, "I just wanted to say thank you for taking care of Wag and Lightfoot and the others."

"My pleasure," replied Harold. He was looking in confusion at the spot where the glittering sparks had been. He saw only Missy's sleeve.

"I know it's a big job. There are so many animals on the farm," Missy went on, just as Harold said, "Your great-aunt left very specific instructions."

"Anyway, thank you," Missy said again.

Missy had never seen anyone quite like Harold, and Harold had never seen anyone quite like Missy.

Harold reached down to pat Wag's head. "Hello, boy."

"Everything is picked up," announced Melody from between shelves of books. She made a slight effort to raise her voice. "Is there anything else I can do, Harold?"

Harold looked outside. "It's such a lovely day. Thank you for the offer, but why don't you go play with your friends?"

"No. That's okay," mumbled Melody.

The door sneezed loudly then, and in walked a boy and a girl about Melody's age. "Hello, Tulip. Hello, Rusty," Harold greeted them.

Missy watched as Melody's eyes grew wide, and she picked her way toward the back of the store. She looked like a crook in a cartoon, tiptoeing away from a crime scene, shoulders hunched, lifting her feet high as if she were marching.

"Where are you going, Melody?" asked Missy.

Melody ignored her. She tiptoed through the biography section.

"Tulip and Rusty Goodenough," said Harold, "meet Missy Piggle-Wiggle. Missy is staying in the upside-down house."

"Huh," said Tulip.

"We thought Mrs. Piggle-Wiggle would be here forever," added Rusty, speaking to his shoes.

"Don't you worry. Things are a bit different now,

but Mrs. Piggle-Wiggle will be back," said Missy cheerfully. She left Wag with Harold and made her way through the store. "Melody?" she called. "Come say hi to Tulip and Rusty. Melody?" She saw no one between the stacks of books. She cracked open the door to the storeroom and peeked inside. No Melody. She opened the back door and looked into the alley. "Melody?" she called again.

Missy looked up and down every aisle in the store. It was when she returned to the front of the store and was talking with Harold and the Goodenough children that she caught sight of Melody walking briskly along Juniper Street in the direction of her home.

Aha, thought Missy. Here was a problem to be solved. Missy had a growing to-do list in her head, and now she added *Think up Shyness Cure for Melody* to it. The cure might not be in the form of a potion. Not everyone needed a potion. But the exact right thing must be thought of to help Melody Flowers.

Missy turned her attention to other matters. "Does anyone know where Merriweather Court is?" she asked. "I need to pay a call on the Freeforalls."

"*Those* kids?" said Rusty. He snorted unattractively.

"Should I be worried?" asked Missy.

"I would if I were you" was Tulip's answer. "They're grabby and loud. They're wild."

"Honoriah is a know-it-all," said Rusty.

"Petulance is greedy," said Tulip.

"Frankfort doesn't care about anything in the whole world," said Rusty. "The whole wide world."

"Goodness," said Missy. "I'd better be on my way."

3
The Freeforalls

IT WAS A warm Saturday afternoon, and Mrs. Hudson Freeforall was trying to enjoy the nice weather. She sat at the desk in her home office and breathed in the late spring smells that wafted through the open window. From her comfortable leather chair, she could see the last of the azalea blooms on the bush outside the window and hear the gentle call of a mourning dove. How anyone can appreciate nice weather while working at a desk is baffling. And why anyone would choose to sit behind her desk on a Saturday, which is a perfectly good weekend day, is even more baffling. But that's exactly what Mrs. Freeforall was doing. Also, she was recalling fondly the spring Saturdays of her youth when she and her older sister would sit on their porch and pursue quiet activities such as making clothes for their dolls or building dollhouse furniture out of toothpicks.

Mrs. Freeforall turned away from the window and back to her computer. She tapped a few keys, then shuffled through a stack of papers on the desk. She was just reaching for her phone when she heard a loud crash, saw a basketball sail through the window and slam into a table, and watched splinters of glass shower onto her lovely, recently vacuumed Oriental carpet. The pictures on the table tumbled off, and one landed on Muffet, the cat, who yowled and ran from the room with a fat tail.

Mrs. Freeforall said nothing. She let out a sigh—a very loud one—and walked to the window, where she stood gazing speculatively into the yard. In her youth (Mrs. Freeforall thought often of her youth), she and her sister always played peacefully. They were cooperative (everyone said so), they remembered their pleases and thank-yous, and they were never loud or messy or rude. They were like little princesses.

Her own children, on the other hand—her dear Honoriah and Petulance and Frankfort—could be referred to only as ruffians. They were responsible for the basketball that had just plunged through her window, but they weren't going to own up to it. They had already run off.

Children today, Mrs. Freeforall reflected, so rarely took responsibility for their own actions. At any rate, *her* children rarely took responsibility for their actions.

Mrs. Freeforall saw Honoriah's bicycle lying on its side, the wheels still spinning. She saw a flowerpot that had been upended, the sad geranium now splayed on the lawn, roots and all, wilting in the sun. She saw a book in a puddle and the wrappers from granola bars flapping about in the breeze.

The yard looked as though a troop of gorillas had charged through it.

Mrs. Freeforall thought of the charming and respectful children who lived next door, Della and Peony LaCarte. Della and Peony were never rude or grabby or noisy. They were courteous and conscientious and tidy.

They were forbidden to play with the Freeforalls.

How had the LaCartes managed to raise such

angels? That was what Mrs. Freeforall had wondered the previous weekend when she had also been working at her desk, and when her husband had been working at *his* desk in the next room, which was *his* office. Their children had been banging on the office doors, demanding that their parents come out and play with them, and Mrs. Freeforall had thought, *I can't get a lick of work done with all this noise and commotion. How did the LaCartes ever raise such angels?*

But that was not what had prompted her to call Mrs. Piggle-Wiggle. No, she had put through her call to Mrs. Piggle-Wiggle a week before *that*, after her dear children had decided to play tattoo parlor and had given one another large tattoos—spider's webs, fake black eyes, skulls, mustaches—in black ink that turned out to be indelible, which is a fancy word for permanent. The Freeforalls had been forced to send their children off to school and out into the world in general looking like the hooligans they were.

After that, Della and Peony were not even permitted to walk to school with them.

Mrs. Piggle-Wiggle had said she thought she knew

just the cure for such children but that she wanted to think things through. She promised to call Mrs. Freeforall back, but Mrs. Freeforall hadn't heard from her. She had heard, however—from Mrs. LaCarte, who was the one who had given Mrs. Freeforall Mrs. Piggle-Wiggle's number in the first place—that the magic lady with the potions for children had been called away and that her great-niece was coming to stay in the upside-down house.

This was the thought that was going through Mrs. Hudson Freeforall's mind as she stood surveying the basketball and the shards of glass: that Mrs. Piggle-Wiggle was gone and apparently for a long time. Mrs. Piggle-Wiggle had been Mrs. Freeforall's one hope for her children. She didn't know *what* she was supposed to do now.

And then the doorbell rang.

Mrs. Freeforall closed the door to her office behind her, noting that she must go in there with the vacuum later and clean up the mess. She was on her way to the front of the house when she heard pounding feet and shrill cries as her children stampeded for the door. The last time she'd seen them, they'd been in the backyard. She wanted very much to think that they had come inside to apologize for throwing the basketball through the window, but she couldn't remember the last time her children had apologized for anything.

She listened to their voices.

"I want to answer the door! It's *my* turn!" That was Petulance.

"No, it isn't. It's my turn! You had a turn this morning!" That was Honoriah.

"I don't care what you girls say; *I'm* going to answer the door!" That was Frankfort.

"No, me!"

"No, me!"

"No, me!"

Mrs. Freeforall, who was getting a headache, couldn't even tell which of her children was yelling now. The yelling was soon accompanied by three thumps as the children, one by one, ran into the door. Their mother hurried into the front hallway just in time to see all three children grab for the doorknob, wrench it around, and pull the door open with such force that they fell backward onto the floor.

"Goodness me."

This was spoken by the woman standing on the Freeforalls' stoop.

Mrs. Hudson Freeforall stepped around her children and said, "Yes?"

The woman was wearing a straw hat. Strands of wild red hair poked out from beneath it, as if nothing at all could contain it. She was wearing a strange blue outfit, and she was holding a leash, at the other end of which was a pleasant-looking dog whose tail was wagging, even though he was sitting down.

Mrs. Freeforall stared at the woman. Was she . . . glowing?

"Are you the Freeforalls?" asked the woman.

The children righted themselves. "Who are you?" was their reply.

"You'll have to excuse them," said their mother. "Yes, we are the Freeforalls. And you are?"

"I'm Missy Piggle-Wiggle. My great-aunt left—"

Missy had thought she would need to offer a lengthy explanation as to why she had dropped by, but Mrs. Freeforall let out an enormous sigh of relief and pulled her inside.

"Oh, thank heavens!" she exclaimed. "I'm at my wit's end. The children are out of—" She stopped speaking abruptly. "Twins, Frankfort, why don't you go up to your rooms for a while?"

"No," said Petulance.

"Why should we?" asked Frankfort.

"We can eavesdrop better from down here," said Honoriah.

Missy looked at the children. She raised her eyebrows. Honoriah, Frankfort, and Petulance ran up the stairs.

"My!" exclaimed their mother. "I've never seen them do that before." She listened to the silence in the house. Extraordinary.

Mrs. Freeforall led Missy into the living room, where they sat down and Wag fell asleep.

"The thing is," Mrs. Freeforall began, "I called your great-aunt a while ago for help with the children. As you can see they're a bit . . . difficult." She thought fleetingly of the mustache tattoos and the yard that looked like an ape pen. "Mrs. LaCarte next door suggested that a touch of magic—a potion or tonic—from your great-aunt might be helpful. I don't suppose that *you*—"

"We're cut from the same cloth," said Missy.

Mrs. Freeforall nodded and looked very relieved. "The worst of it," she went on, "is that we have a sitter who comes in Tuesday and Thursday afternoons to watch the children after school. But she recently gave notice that she'll be leaving in a couple of weeks."

"I see," said Missy, recalling the commotion that had greeted the ringing of the doorbell.

Mrs. Freeforall had the feeling that Missy truly did see, that she understood everything, and she felt grateful that she wouldn't have to go into any more detail about her children's unruly behavior.

A crash came from somewhere above, followed by a shout of "Give it back!"

Mrs. Freeforall rubbed at her aching temples.

Missy said, "I'll take it."

"What?"

"I'll take the job. Tuesday and Thursday afternoons for the foreseeable future." The Freeforalls were going to be a lot of work, and Missy would need plenty of time with them.

"Well, that's—that's wonderful."

"Now to start, I'll need some information about the children."

"Oh, they're lovely," said Mrs. Freeforall. "Really. I mean, they're *capable* of being lovely." She paused. "Honoriah and Petulance are twins. Identical, as you could see. They're nine. And Frankfort is seven. My husband and I work long hours, and we travel a lot, too. We have offices here at the house so that we can work at home in addition to going into the city."

"What are the children's schedules?" asked Missy.

"Their schedules?"

"What do they do on Tuesday and Thursday afternoons when I'll be here?"

Mrs. Freeforall scrunched up her face and thought. "Whatever children do, I suppose."

"What are their interests, then?"

"Oh, they play in the yard," said Mrs. Freeforall vaguely. "They ride their bicycles and . . . Well, really, they're allowed to do whatever they want. We don't have any rules here. Except that the children must go to school. They must do that!" she added brightly.

"Of course," murmured Missy. "And what about meals?"

Mrs. Freeforall once again looked puzzled. "There's plenty of food in the kitchen," she said at last. "They know where everything is."

Missy stood up abruptly. She adjusted her hat, which was listing to the side. "I believe I have enough information," she said.

Mrs. Freeforall looked helplessly up at her. "I know my husband and I run the household a bit loosely. It's just that we spend so much time working. We don't want to be strict with the children on top of everything else. We want them to have fun."

"That's perfectly understandable," said Missy. "Could I spend some time alone with them before I leave? I'd like to get acquainted with them."

When Mrs. Freeforall called for the twins and Frankfort, they came barreling down the stairs just as noisily as you might imagine.

Honestly, thought their mother. *They sound like cattle.*

"Yeah?" said Frankfort as he reached the bottom of the steps.

"What do you want?" asked Honoriah and Petulance.

"Missy is going to be your new babysitter," announced their mother.

This was greeted by groans so loud that Wag woke up and began to slink from the room, tail between his legs.

Missy waited for the children's mother to admonish them. But Mrs. Freeforall simply smiled indulgently at her brood.

Missy clapped her hands together. "Let's go outside," she said.

"Right now?" whined Petulance.

"With *you*?" said Frankfort.

"Do we have to?" asked Honoriah.

"Yes, yes, and yes," replied Missy. "Frankfort, you start the parade. Wag and I will bring up the rear."

"Rear!" hooted Petulance. "She said *rear*!"

But Frankfort said, "I like parades," and set off through the kitchen waving an imaginary baton. His sisters fell into place behind him. They walked sullenly along as though they had weights in their shoes, until

Missy cried, "Use your imaginations!" Then the twins became musicians and played invisible instruments until everyone had marched into the yard and gathered around the picnic table.

"Now," said Missy. "Let me see what I have here."

"Have where?" asked Honoriah.

"Right here." Missy shrugged her shoulder, and suddenly a red satchel appeared on the table, fastened with all sorts of interesting buckles and snaps and ties.

"Ooh," said Frankfort. "What's that?"

"Where did it come from?" asked Honoriah.

"Can I open it?" asked Petulance. She grabbed it without waiting for an answer. "Let *me* open it." And she did.

What spilled onto the table was the biggest collection of art supplies the Freeforall children had ever seen. Tubes of glitter, bundles of markers, packages of pipe cleaners and pom-poms and sequins, bottles of glue, stacks of paper, yarn and feathers and stamps and ink pads.

"Whoa," whispered Petulance.

"I still don't get where it came from," said Honoriah. "You weren't carrying anything."

"Who cares?" asked Frankfort. He reached for the tube of blue glitter—one of seven tubes of glitter—and Petulance smacked his hand away.

"I want that one!" she cried.

Missy removed a small book from her purse and wrote a note to herself.

"What's that? Your spy notebook?" asked Honoriah.

"Personal business," said Missy crisply.

"What are we supposed to do with all this stuff?" asked Honoriah, surveying the table.

"My goodness. Haven't you ever used your imaginations? Why don't you make crowns? Today we are all royalty."

"Even him?" asked Frankfort, pointing to Wag.

"His name is Wag, and yes, even Wag. Today we are kings and queens, and Wag is His Royal Dogness."

"Ha!" exclaimed Honoriah. "His Royal Dogness. *Dogness* isn't even a real word. You just made that up."

"I most certainly did. Now let's get to work."

"How do you make a crown?" Frankfort asked Missy.

"You start with gold paper, of course," said Honoriah. "Everyone knows that."

Petulance pulled a stack of gold paper in front of her.

"Hey!" cried Honoriah. "You can't have it all."

"But I need it all."

"Hog!" said Frankfort, grabbing the stack.

"Frankfort," said Missy, "when you call someone a name, you hurt her feelings."

"I don't care. She *is* being a hog."

Petulance grabbed the paper back. "Mine!"

Suddenly three pairs of hands were pulling at the papers. And just like that, the paper—the entire stack—disappeared. Petulance, who had been grabbing the most fiercely, fell forward onto the table.

"Hey! Who did that?" Frankfort turned accusingly to Missy.

"I think," said Missy, "that each of you needs just two pieces of gold paper." Two sheets appeared in front of each Freeforall.

Wordlessly, the children set to work. Frankfort carefully cut his papers into points.

Honoriah stared at him. Finally she exclaimed, "That's not how you do it!"

"Whatever. That's how I do it. Work on your own crown."

From the end of the table, Missy muttered, "Whatever," and made another notation in her book.

"La, la, la," hummed Petulance as she worked. "I am the Queen of Everything. In fact, that's going to be my royal name. Petulance, Queen of Everything."

"How can you be the Queen of Everything?" asked Honoriah. "That's impossible."

Missy made another notation in her book: *know-it-all.*

She looked down at Wag, who rested at her feet, his front paws lined up neatly. The afternoon sun shone on the table, and for a while the Freeforalls worked silently.

"Ready to decorate," said Petulance presently, and she opened her arms and swept as many of the supplies to her spot at the table as she could manage.

Missy opened her notebook again. This time she wrote, *on the greedy side.*

Twenty minutes later, the Royal Freeforalls sat at the table wearing their crowns. Honoriah had declared herself the Queen of Smartness.

"Who are you?" Missy asked Frankfort.

"Nobody," he replied. He shrugged his shoulders.

"Whatever." He dashed around the yard in his crown, grabbed a handful of pebbles, and began bouncing them off Wag's back. "Come on and play with me, dog," he said.

Wag turned mournful eyes to Missy.

"Come on, dog! Come on, dog!" Frankfort took a step toward Wag, who rose to his feet and ran away. Frankfort followed him.

He almost bumped into Missy—that was how quickly she appeared in front of him.

"Wag does not like what you're doing," said Missy. Her hands were on her hips. "And please use his name when you talk to him."

Frankfort stopped in his tracks. For just a moment he felt as though he couldn't move his feet. He teetered in place. He lifted one foot, then the other. He found that they worked fine. "Sorry," he said, and checked his feet again.

At the picnic table, the Queen of Everything and the Queen of Smartness had stopped what they were doing and were staring at Missy. Then Petulance bonked Honoriah on the head and bent her crown, and Honoriah began to cry. Missy got out her notebook again.

Later, as Missy and Wag walked back to the upside-down house, Missy thought about the Freeforalls. She thought about her cabinet full of cures and of the notes she had made to herself that afternoon.

"We'll need a Greediness Cure," she said to Wag. "That's for Petulance. And a Know-It-All Cure for Honoriah, and for Frankfort, a Whatever Cure. Oh, and the Shyness Cure for Melody. I'd better get to work."

Missy began to whistle as she walked along. Then she began to skip, just a little. Wag gave her a doggy grin.

"It's lovely to be back in Little Spring Valley," said Missy, and she began to plan her cures.

4

The I-Never-Said-That Cure

IT WAS ANOTHER bright Saturday morning in Little Spring Valley. Missy stood in the shower and let the warm water wash over her. She had just gotten her hair nicely foamed up with lemony shampoo when she heard Penelope screech, "Georgie Pepperpot is here!"

Missy jumped. She wasn't yet used to having visitors loudly announced by Penelope and did not recall this from her childhood visits to the upside-down house. She found Penelope much more startling than Harold Spectacle's sneezing door.

"Invite him in!" Missy called back. "But please ask Georgie to stay downstairs until I'm dressed."

"All righty," Penelope replied.

"Tell him there's gingerbread in the kitchen."

"Okeydoke."

Missy finished her shower in a hurry, rinsing the soap out of her hair and reaching for her hat and the green flowered dress she'd hung on the back of the bathroom door. She wished Penelope wouldn't start these loud conversations with her. She was forced to admit people to her house in all sorts of situations—when she was on the telephone or napping. Or taking a shower. There was no pretending she wasn't at home.

Still, Missy was delighted to learn that Georgie Pepperpot had dropped by. When she was growing up, children had trooped in and out of her great-aunt's house every single day. But since she'd arrived in town, she'd been visited by only Tulip and Rusty Good-enough, Beaufort Crumpet, and Melody—and Tulip and Beaufort had made it clear that they'd dropped by to visit Wag and Lightfoot, not Missy.

"When's your aunt coming back?" Beaufort had asked pointedly. He was chewing on a wad of bright pink bubble gum, and a lollipop was sticking out of one pocket.

"Yeah, how long are *you* going to be here?" Tulip had added.

Missy had tried not to feel hurt by the questions and had said instead, "Wag and Lightfoot certainly do enjoy your company."

"That's because they probably miss—"

Missy cut off Beaufort's rude remark with, "You're very good with animals."

Beaufort hadn't been expecting a compliment and wasn't certain how to reply, so he said nothing. But Missy noted that he returned to the upside-down house the next day, this time with his friend Linden Pettigrew, and that the boys spent a good deal of time inside with Missy, sliding down the banister, vaulting over the tops of doorways, and begging her to make gingerbread.

Now Missy, still barefoot after her shower, hustled downstairs and found Georgie seated at the kitchen table with Lester. In front of each of them was a plate of gingerbread. Lester, whose back legs were neatly crossed under the table, cut a small bite from his piece of gingerbread and moved it daintily to his snout with a fork. He chewed delicately, his mouth closed. Between bites he took sips from a cup of coffee.

Georgie shoveled his cake into his mouth using his fingers and then wiped his hands on his shirt. Lester flapped a napkin in his direction, but Georgie ignored it. Still, Missy was happy that Georgie had dropped by. She was just wondering whether it was the perfect day for a game of pirates or the perfect day for a game of trolls and gnomes when Penelope squawked, "Missy, Veronica Cupcake is here!"

"Thank you," called Missy.

She hurried from the kitchen and reached the hall in time to see the house admit a tiny girl of five or six with red ribbons tied at the ends of her braids. (Missy was careful not to use the term *pigtail*, since Lester found it offensive.) The girl was wearing a red dress and red sneakers and holding out a gift in a red bag.

"This is for you," she said to Missy.

"Why, thank you."

"It's to say . . ." Veronica trailed off and scrunched up her face as if she were trying to remember something. "To say welcome to Little Spring Valley." She handed the bag to Missy. "It's cookies," she added. "We bought them at the store, and my mother got a parking ticket."

"My," said Missy. "Well, come into the kitchen and—"

"Missy, Melody Flowers is here!" Penelope announced.

And that was how the morning went. Children kept arriving. Some ignored Missy and wanted to know when Mrs. Piggle-Wiggle planned on returning. Others greeted Missy with hugs and asked whether it would be all right to dig for treasure or build a time machine or make macaroni jewelry. The gingerbread was eaten up, and Missy and Veronica made another batch. Tulip and two friends made a large mess out in the barn but returned to say that they had given Wag a bath.

It was just before lunchtime when Missy noticed the problem with Georgie and a case of I-Never-Said-itis. At first she barely paid it any attention. This was because she was paying more attention to Melody, who always seemed to be playing alone. The upside-down house was now a busy place. There were three fresh holes in the front yard where Beaufort and a small gang of boys were digging for Mr. Piggle-Wiggle's buried treasure. The kitchen was a flurry of gingerbread-making activity. Two children were turning a cardboard carton into yet another dollhouse, and one of Tulip's friends was trying to teach Veronica how to knit. But Melody was curled up on the end of a couch, reading. Now, reading is a fine activity, of course, but Missy couldn't help but notice that Melody was the only child in the upside-down house who was alone.

She was about to say something to Melody when she heard an argument erupt in the front yard.

"I never said that!"

"Liar! Yes, you did! You did say that. You said it five minutes ago."

Missy hurried to the front door and looked outside. Georgie and Linden were rolling around on the ground, yanking a baseball mitt back and forth.

"What's the problem?" called Missy. She stepped onto the porch.

"There's only one mitt, and Georgie's been hogging it all morning!" cried Linden. Missy noticed that the tips of his ears were turning red.

"It's almost your turn," said Georgie. He stood up, wrenching the mitt away from Linden.

"You said it would be my turn in five minutes. And that was five minutes ago."

"I never said that!"

"Yes, you did, you did! Liar!"

"Land sakes," said Missy. "How about if I take the mitt and you find two bats? I'll pitch to you. Let's see if anyone else wants to play."

~~~~~

Lunch at the upside-down house was, all the children agreed, exactly perfect. It was even as good as if Mrs. Piggle-Wiggle herself had made it. Missy brought special treats in from the garden, and she made sandwiches from homemade bread.

"Who wants orange juice?" Missy asked as the children were finishing their lunches.

"Me!" Petulance Freeforall, who had shown up with Honoriah and Frankfort just before lunch, shot her hand in the air. "But first I want Georgie to show me the secret pirate sign in the oak tree."

"Later," said Georgie.

"But you said you were going to show it to me right away, and then you never did."

"I didn't say that!"

"Actually, you did," said Veronica Cupcake in a serious, grown-up voice.

"No! I never said that."

Missy was beginning to feel just the teensiest bit nervous. I-Never-Said-itis is contagious, and she certainly hoped the other children weren't going to catch it from Georgie. She thought of dinnertime in all the homes in Little Spring Valley, nice peaceful meals suddenly punctuated with loud cries of "I never said that!" She remembered the summer she was twelve years old, visiting Auntie, and nearly every child in town had come down with I-Never-Said-itis. Auntie's phone had rung so often with calls from worn-out parents needing the I-Never-Said-That Cure that finally one day Auntie had had to lie down on the couch with a cold cloth on her head and tell Missy she needed a little break.

It would not do to let things get so out of hand now.

Children must take responsibility for what they say, Missy thought later as she pondered a cure for I-Never-Said-itis. It had been years since the last scourge, and she wondered if the cure might have changed. She thought of the many lessons she had learned from Auntie. *A promise made must be a promise kept.*

It was at that moment that once again Missy heard Georgie exclaim, "I never said that!"

"Yes, you *did!*" The cry was accompanied by

Honoriah's stomping foot. "You said you would trade costumes with me, and now I want to be the Crabby Neighbor. Give me the Crabby Neighbor Hat this instant."

"Later."

"But you *promised*. You said I could—"

"I did not say that."

Missy peeked into the parlor, where the contents of the dress-up box were flung across the floor. Georgie was dressed as an elderly woman. A felt hat with a waving peacock feather was perched on his head.

"I am the crabby old neighbor," he said in a creaky voice. "You kids get out of my yard! Go on! And quit tromping through my flower beds!"

"Georgie?" said Missy. "Did you tell Honoriah she could have a turn with the costume?"

"Nope."

"He did! He did!"

Missy turned and climbed the stairs. She walked down the hallway to her room. Just outside her door, the rug buckled under her feet and she nearly tripped.

"House," she said sternly.

The rug straightened itself.

In her room Missy opened her locket, removed the key, and unlocked the blue cabinet.

"I-Never-Said-itis," she murmured. She surveyed the cures that neatly lined the shelves. She reached for a vial labeled HONESTY, then drew back her hand and instead reached for the jar of Promise Potion. She returned to the kitchen, where she took a heart-shaped cookie from a plate that anyone would have sworn was empty. Then she opened the jar and spread a layer of pink frosting on the cookie.

"Georgie?" she called again. "Could you come here, please?"

"Am I in trouble?" he asked, which, Missy had discovered, was what children often said when they knew they had done something wrong.

"I want to see you for a minute."

Georgie slumped through the kitchen doorway, looking hopeless. "I know, I know," he said. "I have to give Honoriah the Crabby Neighbor Hat."

"If you like," said Missy, "but first I have something special for you." She handed him the cookie. "This is the best cookie you'll ever eat. It will help you keep your promises. I promise."

Georgie ate the cookie in two bites. "Thanks!" he said, and returned to the dress-up box in the parlor. Georgie realized that his stomach felt strangely warm. He sniffed his hands, which smelled a little like cinnamon, and licked at a blot of frosting on his thumb. The warmth spread up through his chest and all the way to his forehead. It wasn't an unpleasant feeling.

Georgie removed the Crabby Neighbor costume (Honoriah snatched up the hat), and he stood in front of the box, deciding whether he'd like to be a sailor or a bug next.

"Hey, Georgie," called Beaufort from the porch. "Come on outside and help us dig!"

"Okay, I'll be right there," replied Georgie, and he continued to contemplate the bug costume. He was reaching for the bobbling antennae when his feet were suddenly whisked out from beneath him, and he found himself sailing through the parlor and out the front door headfirst, as if he'd been launched from a cannon. Then he was dropped to the ground next to Beaufort and Linden. His hands clasped themselves around a shovel, and he began digging energetically.

"What—" cried Georgie.

His friends stared at him, mouths open.

Georgie's arms pumped up and down, up and down. Dirt sprayed from the hole and piled itself up at an alarming rate.

"Whoa," said Linden. "I never saw anyone dig like that before."

Georgie was growing breathless. The hole was a foot deep, then two. When Georgie could no longer reach the bottom, he was pulled down inside, arms still pumping.

"His arms are moving so fast, I can't even see him anymore," exclaimed Beaufort. "He's a blur."

"Hey, Georgie!" Linden cupped his hands and shouted down into the hole, which now measured nearly five feet. "Come on out. I don't think there's any treasure in there. You would have found it by now."

"Okay," puffed Georgie, who was just thinking that he had absolutely no idea how to get out of the hole when he was whooshed straight up and deposited on the pile of earth he'd created.

He slid down and brushed himself off, realizing that his arms ached.

"Georgie, that was so cool," said Linden. "Can you show me how to do that?"

"Um, sure."

Linden stood looking expectantly at Georgie, who was about to add, "Maybe I'll show you tomorrow," not meaning it at all, when he found the shovel in his hands again. "You start like this," Georgie heard a voice say. It took a moment before he realized it was his own. "You pick up the shovel and stick it in the ground."

"Well, I know *that*," said Linden.

"And you heave it up and toss the dirt away, and then you stick it inthegroundandheaveitupandtossthedirtaway." Georgie was speaking faster and faster. "ANDTHENYOUSTICKITINTHEGROUNDANDHEAVEITUPANDTOSSTHEDIRTAWAYANDTHEN—"

"You don't have to yell," said Linden.

Georgie tried to say that he didn't mean to yell, but the words flew uncontrollably from his mouth, faster and louder.

"Stop it! Stop!" Beaufort and Linden put their hands over their ears and ran to the backyard.

The shovel fell from Georgie's hands. He collapsed onto the pile of dirt, closed his eyes, and tried to catch his breath.

"Hey, Georgie, what about the pirate sign?"

Georgie opened his eyes and saw Petulance standing before him. "What about it?"

"Will you show it to me? You said you would."

Georgie hesitated. He felt awfully tired. "I never said that."

Before Petulance could cry, "But you did! You did!" which were the words forming on her lips, Georgie shot up like a rocket and flew to the tallest oak tree in the front yard.

"Hey!" called Petulance. "Wait up! Wait for me!"

"I can't!" Georgie called back. His voice sounded like a motor as he chugged along. "I-I-I-I ca-a-a-a-n't!" He sailed toward the tree, and just when he thought he was going to smack into it, his body righted itself and his arms clasped the trunk. Up he climbed like a monkey—hand, foot, hand, foot—until he was near the very top of the tree.

"Georgie, get down from there! You're going to fall!" cried Petulance.

Georgie looked down at her. All he could see was her upturned face and the tips of her pink sneakers. His hair fell across his eyes, and he tried to brush it away. Instead, his hand pointed to a large knothole in the trunk, and he heard himself yell, "This is it. This is the pirate sign."

There was silence from below. At last Petulance said, "That knothole? *That's* the pirate sign?" She began to suspect that there hadn't been any pirate sign in the first place.

She was right. But Georgie had *said* he would show Petulance a pirate sign, and now he found himself stuck at the top of a tree that was taller than the upside-down house. "Well," said Georgie, clinging to the trunk, which was swaying back and forth, "it *could* be a pirate sign. Doesn't the knothole look like a face?"

"I suppose so," said Petulance, squinting up at him. "How are you going to get down?"

Georgie didn't know, so he said nothing. He was just wondering if he was going to have to bother Missy and ask her to call the fire department when he found himself slipping and sliding back down the tree, almost as if he were being vacuumed down from below. Seconds later, he stood breathlessly on the ground, hands grimy, leaves clinging to his clothes.

"Gosh," said Petulance. "I've never seen anyone do that before."

Georgie thought very carefully before he said, "Me neither."

Petulance left to join the others in the backyard, and Georgie walked thoughtfully to the front porch and sat down, head in his hands.

"Georgie!" called Missy from inside. "I'd like you and Honoriah to come put the dress-up clothes away, please."

"In a minute," Georgie called back. He just needed a small rest.

Sixty seconds later he was still sitting on the porch when he suddenly shot up from the step and hurtled through the front door, which opened all by itself. He whooshed into the parlor, where he found Honoriah picking up hats and shoes and scarves.

"Georgie?" said Honoriah in alarm.

Georgie was too breathless to answer her. His hands scooped up hats and masks and boots and flung them into the dress-up box. When every last item had been put away, his hands reached out again and this time slammed the lid closed. He sat on the box, panting.

Missy appeared in the doorway. "Thank you," she said.

Honoriah backed into the hallway.

Missy crossed her arms and smiled at Georgie.

"I guess I'd better be careful what I say," he ventured. "A minute means a minute."

"And a promise is a promise."

Missy checked her watch. Half an hour had passed since she'd given Georgie the Promise Potion. That was usually all it took. She was sure the potion had worn off by now.

"Would you like to help me in the kitchen?" she asked him. "We could make lemonade with real lemons."

"Sure," Georgie replied. Then he added carefully, "I'll be right there." And he jumped to his feet all on his own and made his way to the kitchen.

5

Petulance Freeforall, or the Greediness Cure

MR. AND MRS. Hudson Freeforall sat at the table in their kitchen early on a Tuesday morning. Honoriah, Petulance, and Frankfort sat with them. For once, all was quiet.

"Isn't this lovely?" asked Mrs. Freeforall, certain that every meal next door at the LaCartes' house was just as peaceful. "All of us together for breakfast, everyone—"

"Give it!" shouted Petulance suddenly. She reached across the table and grabbed at the cinnamon roll Frankfort was holding. "I want that!"

"But I'm *eating* it," exclaimed Frankfort, who had

not in fact started eating it, but now he took a large bite out of the side. "Anyway, I had it first."

"Well, give it. It has extra frosting and I want it."

Frankfort looked incredulously at his parents.

"Dear," Mr. Freeforall said to his wife, "I have an early meeting today, so I'll be going." He stood up and reached for his briefcase.

Petulance stood, too. She leaned over, pulled the remainder of the cinnamon roll out of Frankfort's hands, and stuffed it in her mouth.

"That was mine!" shouted Frankfort.

The Freeforalls didn't eat many meals together, but when they did, Petulance could be counted on to be greedy and grabby, demanding the biggest piece, the ice cream with the most chocolate chips, a drumstick (thank goodness there were two), the reddest strawberries, or the wishbone from the turkey. Petulance always demanded the wishbone and then decided whether Honoriah or Frankfort would get to break it with her. This meant that someone was left out, of course, but it was never Petulance. The last time the Freeforalls had eaten turkey, Hudson Freeforall decided to avoid trouble, and he secretly removed the wishbone and stuffed it down the garbage disposal before Petulance could ask for it.

Mrs. Freeforall watched her husband hurry out the front door. She looked at the remains of the once peaceful breakfast. Crumbs littered the table. A bottle of soda was overturned. Petulance had spilled it after she'd claimed it was hers. "It *is* mine! It *is*!" she had cried. "See? I wrote my name on it."

Her brother and sister leaned in for a look.

"Where?" Honoriah had demanded, clutching the bottle. "I don't see your name."

"I wrote it so tiny it's invisible," Petulance replied. "Now give it." And she'd grabbed it from Honoriah, and of course it had spilled.

Now Honoriah removed a package of gummy worms from the snack cabinet.

"Gummy worms for breakfast?" said her mother wearily.

"Yup," Honoriah replied.

"Hey, how many are left in there?" asked Petulance.

Honoriah thrust the package behind her back. "It's a full bag."

"It is not! I saw it yesterday, and it's almost empty. Give it to me. I want the red ones."

"They all taste the same!"

"Do not."

"Do, too. Don't they, Frankfort?"

"What-*ever.*"

Petulance tackled her sister and pounced on the bag. "Look! It *is* almost empty. You were going to eat them all up, and I want some."

Mrs. Freeforall put her head in her hands. "I need to get to work," she said, "and you need to leave for school."

Twenty minutes later Mrs. Freeforall sat in the quiet of her office, Muffet in her lap. Her computer was turned on, but she was staring blankly at five tropical fish swimming around on the screen. She thought about breakfast. She thought about Petulance. In her mind she saw her grabbing food from her brother and sister. She saw her taking chalk out of poor Peony LaCarte's hand the previous Saturday, in full view of Mr. and Mrs. LaCarte. She saw her in the shoe store, demanding the most expensive shoes in her size simply because they had the most sparkles on them.

At last Mrs. Freeforall made a decision. She reached

for the phone. Before she could pick it up, it rang. She jumped. "Hello?"

"Hello, Mrs. Freeforall? This is Missy Piggle-Wiggle."

"Missy! How odd. I was just about to call you."

"I wanted to confirm that I'll arrive at your house this afternoon at three to begin my job."

"Yes. Oh, *thank you*. Yes," said Mrs. Freeforall. Her head swam with relief. She took a deep breath. "About Petulance," she began. "I'm having a bit of trouble with her. She's just so . . ."

Grabby? thought Missy.

"Willful," offered Mrs. Freeforall limply. "Well, no, that's not quite it."

"She wants what others have?" suggested Missy.

"Yes, exactly. And I wondered if you might have a potion or tonic that could—"

"I know just the thing," said Missy. "I'll bring it with me this afternoon." She refrained from mentioning that the potion, which would simply be mixed into a glass of milk, was in a bottle labeled GREEDINESS CURE.

"Thank you," said Mrs. Freeforall again, sagging

back in her chair. Her computer pinged then, and she hung up the phone abruptly.

"Goodness," murmured Missy. "She didn't even say good-bye."

~~~~~

The three Freeforall children trailed home from school that afternoon behind Peony and Della LaCarte.

"Want to play tattoo parlor?" Frankfort yelled to them.

Della screamed and burst into tears, and Peony shrieked, "Stay off of our property! Please!"

Honoriah waited until she was standing on her own front porch before she shouted back, "No, *you* stay off of *ours*, or I'll call the police and they'll put you in the kids' jail!"

She opened the door, and there were Missy and Wag.

"Oh, it's you, Missy," said Honoriah. "Um, I don't suppose you heard what I was saying to—"

"Come into the kitchen for snack time," Missy interrupted her.

"What are we having?" Frankfort asked. "I want—"

"I made oatmeal cookies," said Missy. She knew how hungry children were when they came home in the afternoon. School schedules often made no sense, and sometimes children had eaten their lunch at ten thirty in the morning.

The Freeforall children rushed into the kitchen and began rummaging through the refrigerator.

"You each have a place at the table," Missy informed them. "Please sit down."

Petulance looked at the table and realized that five places had been set with plates and cups and napkins. There was a name card in front of each plate.

"Honoriah," Petulance read. "Petulance—that's me."

"Duh," said Frankfort.

Petulance ignored him. "Frankfort, Missy, and Wag." She glanced at Missy. "Wag eats at the table?"

"Sometimes. Now take your places."

The Freeforall children slid into their spots. Their cups had been filled with milk. Missy set two oatmeal cookies and four apple slices on each plate.

Petulance reached for her milk and drank it down. She ate both of her cookies and then removed one from Honoriah's plate. "Still hungry," she said.

"Missy!" cried Honoriah indignantly. She was about to add that Petulance hadn't even eaten her fruit, but instead she gasped as the cookie in her sister's hand suddenly became the size of a shirt button.

"Hey!" said Petulance, frowning at her twin. "You take that back."

"Take what back?"

"Whatever you did to my cookie."

"I didn't do anything. And anyway, it was *my* cookie."

Petulance narrowed her eyes but swallowed the teensy cookie. "Mmmm, tasty," she said, even though it was hard to ignore the fact that Frankfort and Honoriah were laughing at her.

"Now," said Missy, watching out of the corner of her eye as Petulance retrieved a bag of chocolate drops from the cupboard and began peeling one, "here's the schedule for this afternoon."

"Why does she get chocolates?" Frankfort cried.

Petulance gave him a smile. "Because I want them."

"You want chocolate crumbs?" asked Honoriah.

The chocolates in Petulance's hand had begun to shrink. She leaned over and peered at them.

"I can barely see them," said Honoriah.

"You're going to need tweezers to peel them," added Frankfort.

"They'll still taste good," said Petulance loftily. "I'll just need to eat more of them." She began using her fingernails to tear at the wrappers.

"As I was saying," said Missy, "the schedule for this afternoon is as follows: Homework time—"

Frankfort erupted from his seat. "*Home*work time?"

"Yes, homework time followed by arts and crafts followed by supervised free time—ten minutes— followed by dinner-prep time."

"What's dinner-prep time?" asked Petulance. She had rummaged around in a drawer until she'd found a magnifying glass, which she'd propped up on the table. Now she was trying to peel the chocolates behind it.

"Wow, your fingers look like giant pink sea worms," Frankfort told her.

"Dinner-prep time," said Missy, "is when we all fix dinner together."

"But—but—" spluttered Honoriah.

"Now clear the table, please," said Missy. "Plates and glasses in the sink."

Reluctantly, the Freeforalls cleared the table and spread out books and work sheets. Honoriah industriously began writing ten sentences in Spanish. "There," she said after a while. "All done."

Petulance reached across the table and took her paper. "Let me copy yours. I can't think of any sentences."

"You haven't even tried," said her sister.

"Hey!" exclaimed Petulance. "I can't read this! What did you do to it?" The paper had become the size of a postage stamp.

"Maybe she used tiny, invisible letters," spoke up Frankfort, "like when you wrote on the soda bottle."

Petulance scowled at him.

Honoriah drew the paper back, and it returned to its proper size. "Thank goodness," she said. "Mrs. Peabody would have given me an F. Now write your own sentences, Petulance."

At six o'clock that evening, Mr. and Mrs. Freeforall returned, briefcases in hand. Honoriah greeted them at the door and exclaimed, "Come look at the dining room!"

Candles were burning, and the table was set with the china that was ordinarily reserved for holidays.

"Doesn't it look like a party?" asked Frankfort.

"We did it all ourselves," added Petulance.

"And we helped make dinner," said Honoriah.

Mr. and Mrs. Freeforall glanced at each other in astonishment.

"Well," said Missy, "Wag and I will be off. We'll see you again on Thursday."

Mrs. Freeforall wanted to say, "No, don't leave!" but just in time she remembered that she was a grown-up.

"What's for dinner?" asked her husband.

"You'll never guess," replied Petulance with excitement. "Turkey!"

"Sliced turkey?" Mr. Freeforall asked her hopefully.

"Nope, a whole turkey. And I claim the wishbone. Oh, and a drumstick!"

Mrs. Freeforall sighed and watched helplessly as Missy and Wag disappeared through the front door.

"Let's eat right now," said Frankfort. "Come on, everybody."

The Freeforalls sat at the table. It was spread with dishes of mashed potatoes and cranberry sauce and peas and olives.

And the turkey.

"I guess I'll carve," said Mr. Freeforall reluctantly.

"Remember, I want a drumstick," announced Petulance.

"So do I," said Honoriah.

To her surprise, Mrs. Freeforall found herself saying, "So do I."

"Well, there are only two," Petulance reminded her unnecessarily. "And I want one." She paused and added, "I WANT one!"

"Settle down," said her father. He sliced off a drumstick and dropped it on Petulance's plate. Then he stared at the plate in astonishment. "What happened? Where's the drumstick?"

All the Freeforalls leaned in for a good look. "Oh, there it is," said Honoriah, whose nose was practically touching the plate. She pointed at a speck by the rim.

"*That's* the drumstick?" asked Mrs. Freeforall.

Petulance picked it up between her thumb and

forefinger as if it were an ant and handed it to her father. "Take it back. I don't want it anymore."

Mr. and Mrs. Freeforall gazed at the drumstick as it crossed the table. By the time it returned to the turkey platter, Mrs. Freeforall thought that it might be even bigger than it had been in the first place. Her husband handed it to her and gave the other one to Honoriah.

"Remember about the wishbone," said Petulance.

"Hard to forget," muttered her father. He continued carving.

Frankfort reached for the olives, but Petulance got to them first and selected the largest one. It disappeared altogether. She pursed her lips and said nothing.

"Have a roll, dear," said her mother, passing her a plate.

"Thanks," said Petulance. Her hand hovered over the fattest, fluffiest one, with the brownest top, and then she took a small one from the side of the plate.

She held her breath. Nothing happened.

Nothing happened when she helped herself to the mashed potatoes, either, not saying a word even though Frankfort had gotten the spoonful with the best lumps.

It was in the kitchen later that evening when trouble erupted. "Carve up the rest of the turkey now, Dad," said Petulance.

"Can't it wait?"

"No, I want the wishbone. Now!" Petulance couldn't help but remember her sad little roll and her boring, lumpless potatoes and the sight of her mother and sister eating the drumsticks.

Mr. Freeforall located the wishbone. "Here it is," he said.

Petulance grabbed it out of his hands. Naturally, it shrank to the size of a hummingbird wishbone. "Well, that doesn't matter," she said. "We can still break it. Frankfort, take the other side."

Frankfort reached out and pinched.

"Ow! That's my finger!" cried Petulance.

"Well, this thing's so tiny, I can't see what I'm doing. Where's the magnifying glass?"

"Oh, never mind. Honoriah, you try."

Honoriah shook her head. "It's too little. Here, let me have it for a second."

Petulance let go of the wishbone, and of course as soon as she did, it returned to its original size.

Her lower lip began to tremble. Hudson Freeforall suddenly felt sorry for his daughter. "You need to let the wishbone dry before you break it anyway," he reminded her. "Let's set it aside for a few days."

Petulance slogged upstairs to her bedroom.

By the next evening, Petulance had a collection of miniature items on her dresser: a half-inch-long barrette she'd taken from Honoriah's room, two jelly dough-nuts that looked like crumbs, and a magazine that had arrived in the mail and was now the size of a fingernail. She had tried turning the pages of the magazine but had given up when she realized the print was too small to read anyway. Next to all these items was the magni-fying glass.

Honoriah entered her sister's room without knock-ing. Petulance was slumped on her bed, her head in her arms.

"What's the matter?" asked her twin.

Petulance shrugged.

"Do you know where my barrette is?"

Petulance pointed to her dresser. "I took it. Sorry. You can have it back. In fact, you can have everything there."

"Really? Even the magazine? You always like to

read it first." Honoriah peered at it. "It *is* the magazine, isn't it?"

"Yeah. You can read it first today. We might as well take turns anyway."

And just like that, the minuscule magazine inflated to its proper size, and another magazine appeared in Petulance's hands.

"Hey, one for each of us! Thanks, Petulance," said Honoriah.

The next morning Petulance announced that she was going to have a Popsicle for breakfast, and since her parents didn't stop her, she opened the freezer.

"Get me one, too," said Frankfort.

At this, Mrs. Freeforall let out a groan. She knew there was only one Popsicle in the freezer, and she foresaw a fight.

To her mother's surprise, Petulance withdrew the remaining Popsicle and handed it to Frankfort. "Here," she said. As she turned to close the door, a second Popsicle floated out of the freezer and landed on her plate.

This was when Mrs. Freeforall remembered Missy Piggle-Wiggle and her potions, and once again she was flooded with relief.

"Petulance, that was very nice of you," she said, and gave her daughter a hug.

Petulance smiled. "I was thinking," she said to Honoriah and Frankfort. "Tonight if the wishbone is dry, you two can pull it. I've had lots of turns."

"Really?" said her brother and sister.

"*Really?*" said her father.

Petulance nodded.

"In that case," said Honoriah, "tell me your wish and I'll make it for you."

Hudson Freeforall looked as though he might faint. His wife hurried to his place at the table. "It's Missy Piggle-Wiggle," she whispered to him. "She really is magic."

The Freeforall parents listened to the happy chatter about the wishbone, and even though their children were eating Popsicles for breakfast and their hair was unbrushed and Frankfort's hand was bandaged because he'd ridden a skateboard into the kitchen wall the evening before, Mr. and Mrs. Hudson Freeforall felt hopeful.

6

The Tardiness Cure

MR. HAMILTON EARWIG looked at the ringing phone on the desk in his downtown office and sighed when he saw that the caller ID read LSV ELEMENTARY SCHOOL. He didn't even have to check his watch to know that the time must be near three o'clock. He already knew who would be on the line and what he would be calling about.

He held the phone to his ear. "Mr. Bovine?" he asked.

"Good afternoon, Mr. Earwig. I wanted to—"

"Don't tell me," said Mr. Earwig. He knew he sounded rude, but he couldn't help it. This was the fourth time in less than a month that Mr. Bovine had called to say that Heavenly Earwig had missed her bus home. "I'll be there as soon as I can."

Mr. Earwig hung up the phone and fumed and muttered to himself for several moments. "No respect for anyone," he mumbled. "You'd think she never learned to tell time." He picked up a pile of papers and slapped them back down onto his desk. "Rude and thoughtless."

Mr. Earwig pictured Heavenly on the day she'd been born. She had been so beautiful and so sweet that he and his wife, who had planned to name their daughter Bertha, had changed their minds and named her Heavenly instead. And Heavenly had been heavenly right up until she turned ten. Then a change had come over her, and the Earwigs' perfect little girl had become scatterbrained and absentminded, not to mention a dawdler and a daydreamer.

"She's just imaginative," the Earwigs had assured each other at first.

"I've heard that creative people are like this," Mrs. Earwig had added.

"Smart people, too," said Mr. Earwig. "I believe Einstein was absentminded."

"Really?" asked his wife.

"I don't know."

Heavenly's fifth-grade report cards certainly didn't reflect great intelligence.

"Straight Ds!" Mrs. Earwig had cried when she'd seen the first report card of the year. "Heavenly, what happened?"

"Huh?" said Heavenly, who had been thinking what fun it would be to have a pet possum. A giant flying possum that could give her rides around the neighborhood.

"How did you manage to get straight *Ds*?"

Heavenly tried to stop thinking about the flying possum. "Oh, that. Keep reading," she said.

Mrs. Earwig skimmed farther down Mr. Bovine's comments. "You were late handing in your homework twenty-seven times?" she asked her daughter.

"Huh?" said Heavenly again. She was thinking that a possum that could drive would be even better.

"Heavenly!" exclaimed her mother.

Heavenly jerked to attention. "I handed it in eventually."

"But you were late twenty-seven times?"

"I guess so."

Recently Mr. and Mrs. Earwig had spent many evenings having a conversation that went something like this:

"She missed the school bus again today."

"Morning or afternoon?"

"Both."

"Yesterday she slept through her alarm. Then I had to call her sixteen times before she got out of bed."

"I hope Cramden doesn't turn out this way." (Cramden was Heavenly's one-year-old brother.)

Now Mr. Earwig drummed his fingers on the steering wheel in annoyance as, once again, he drove to Little Spring Valley Elementary School to pick up Heavenly.

He found her squatting on the ground by a bench in front of the school. She was the only student in sight.

"Heavenly!" he called.

Heavenly was staring intently at an ant in the grass, thinking that if humans had the strength of ants, they could carry boulders and apartment buildings around on their backs.

"Heavenly!"

Heavenly jumped. "You don't have to be so loud,

Dad," she said. She hefted her backpack and ambled toward the car.

"HEAVENLY!"

Heavenly picked up her pace. "Why are you yelling?" She opened the door and slid inside.

Mr. Earwig counted to ten and reminded himself that he was thirty-two years older than his daughter. He took a deep breath and let it out slowly. "I'm yelling," he said carefully, "because I had to leave work to pick you up when you could have taken the bus home. Why did you miss the bus?" He almost added "again," but he didn't want to seem unnecessarily cruel.

"I lost track of the time."

"How could you lose track of the time? School was over. Surely you knew you were supposed to get on the bus then. Weren't all your friends getting on their buses?"

"I guess."

Heavenly hadn't been paying attention to her friends. She had happened to walk by the nurse's office on the way to her locker and had peeked inside and seen Mrs. Pazden helping a boy who had broken his finger. Heavenly had never seen a broken finger before, so she had stopped to watch. And then, in her locker she had found an essay she'd written on the first day of school and had decided to reread it. After that, she had noticed that the hallway was empty and had gone outside to find her bus, but the buses had left, and then she had noticed the ant.

Heavenly tried to explain this to her father.

He shook his head.

That night Heavenly was late to dinner. Mrs. Earwig called her and called her and called her. "Coming!" Heavenly replied each time, her voice floating out of her bedroom.

But she didn't come.

Mr. and Mrs. Earwig looked at each other across the dining room table. Cramden patted his fists on the tray of his high chair and squawked.

"The food's getting cold," remarked Mrs. Earwig. "What on earth is Heavenly doing? You call her this time, dear."

"Heavenly!!" roared her father.

"Coming!"

The Earwigs sat at the table for ten more minutes. Some of the food got crusty around the edges.

Eventually, Heavenly sauntered down the stairs. She put a forkful of chicken in her mouth. "Hey, this is cold," she said. "Is something wrong with the oven?"

When dinner was over and Cramden had been put to bed, Mr. and Mrs. Earwig sat together in the living room with cups of coffee. Heavenly was in her room doing her homework.

"At least, I hope she's doing it," said her mother. "She was supposed to start it before supper, but I found her up there with her colored pencils drawing a family with twenty-two children." She paused. "That could take a while."

Mr. Earwig closed his eyes briefly. Then he said, "Something must be done."

"We don't want to stifle her creativity."

"There's nothing creative about cold chicken. I was talking to Lavinia Foxtrot at the office this afternoon, and she told me that her Elvira got a certificate at school for handing in every single one of her homework assignments on time."

"Well," said Mrs. Earwig, "anyone can be punctual."

"Not Heavenly."

There was silence in the room. At last Mr. Earwig

said, "I've been hearing wonderful things about Mrs. Piggle-Wiggle's great-niece. Don't you think it's time we called her?"

"Oh, Hamilton. I don't know."

"Tomorrow is your day to drive Heavenly to school if she misses the bus," he reminded her.

Mrs. Earwig handed her husband the phone. "All right," she said.

Hamilton dialed the phone so quickly that his wife decided—correctly—that he had already looked up Missy's number and memorized it.

"Is this Missy?" asked Hamilton when the phone was answered. He knew that a talking parrot lived at the upside-down house, and he wanted to make sure he had Missy herself on the phone.

"It is."

"This is Mr. Earwig. I'm calling about a problem with my daughter."

"Heavenly?" asked Missy. "Why, she's lovely."

"Yes, but she's having some difficulty being on time."

"Late for meals?" asked Missy. "Missing the bus? Trouble getting up in the morning?"

"All those things," said Mr. Earwig. "My wife and I were wondering if you knew of—"

"I certainly do. The Tardiness Cure. It works fast. Very effective. Tell Heavenly to drop by my house tomorrow after school. I have a special watch for her."

The next day Heavenly managed to catch the bus both to and from school, but it took her nearly half an hour to walk the five blocks to Missy's house that afternoon because she kept stopping to sit on the curb and think up names for the twenty-two children in her imaginary family. At last she reached the porch of the upside-down house. She rang the bell.

"Missy, Heavenly Earwig is here!" Penelope announced.

Missy answered the door wearing a long gown and a gingham bonnet since she was playing dress-up with Melody. She handed a wristwatch to Heavenly, who stared at it. "What am I supposed to do with it?" she asked.

"Just keep it with you at all times."

Heavenly shrugged. "Okay." She put the watch on and felt it vibrating lightly on her wrist.

She thanked Missy, ambled down the porch steps,

and walked along the path to the sidewalk, noticing that there was a cloud in the sky that looked almost exactly like a baby monkey. At the sidewalk, Heavenly turned right instead of left so that she could take the long route home and play at Harry's Brook for a while. She had once seen a quarter shining in the water, and while she was fishing it out, she had found a nickel as well.

Heavenly made her way to the brook, stopping four times to name some more of her children. When she reached the little bridge over the brook, she stepped off the sidewalk and slid down the bank until she was standing with the water lapping at the toes of her sneakers.

Ahead of her the sun hung low in the sky, turning the water a brilliant orange. Heavenly thought of the prospectors during the gold rush. Surely they couldn't have found every single piece of gold in the whole country. There must be one or two somewhere in Harry's Brook. She stood up and leaned over, shading her eyes from the sun.

The noise that filled the air then was so sudden and so deafeningly loud that Heavenly nearly pitched forward into the water. She righted herself just in time and leaped backward, clapping her hands over her ears to shut out the sound of a thousand bells gonging and a million phones ringing all at the same time.

In a tree branch above her head, a sparrow perched peacefully.

"Don't you hear that?" Heavenly shouted over the din.

The sparrow ruffled its feathers and closed its eyes. It looked sleepy.

On the bridge above, Frankfort Freeforall stood looking down at Heavenly. "What are you yelling for?" he called.

Heavenly cupped her hand to her ear. "What? I can't hear you over all that noise."

"What noise?"

"Are you kidding me? That—that *ringing* sound."

Frankfort shook his head at her and continued on his way.

Heavenly happened to glance at the watch then. "Almost six o'clock!" she exclaimed. "It's dinnertime. I'm supposed to be home in a few minutes."

She ran the rest of the way to her house with her fingers in her ears. As she ran, she noticed all the peaceful people around her. People calmly sitting on their porches or watering their lawns. People chatting, people driving slowly along the street. She didn't see a single person with his or her fingers plugging his or her ears.

Heavenly reached her house and tore through the front door. She slid into her place at the table just as her father set down a bowl of spaghetti and her mother plopped Cramden into his high chair.

Mr. and Mrs. Earwig looked at each other in astonishment. "You're on time," they said.

"I am?" Heavenly replied, and the noise stopped.

In the sudden silence, Heavenly nearly fell out of her chair. "What's that?" she said. Her ears were still ringing.

"What's what?" asked her mother.

"You didn't hear anything?"

"Hear what?"

"Nothing. Never mind."

"Did you get to Missy's house all right?" asked Mr. Earwig.

"Yup. Just fine."

Mr. Earwig served up the spaghetti, and Mrs. Earwig passed around a salad.

"Hey, the spaghetti's hot tonight," said Heavenly. "Nice going, Mom."

Before she went to bed, Heavenly carefully placed her new watch on the nightstand and set it to go off at six thirty the next morning. So she was confused and startled to be awakened at four o'clock by a jangling sound that seemed to bounce off the walls of her room.

Clang, clang. Bong, bong. CLANG, CLANG! BONG, BONG!

Heavenly scrambled out of bed and tapped on her watch, but the noise only grew louder. She opened the door to her room and waited for the sight of her parents running groggily down the hall, or for the sound of Cramden bawling in his crib. But her family slumbered on. Back in her room, she pulled up her window shade and looked out at Dogwood Lane. Just as suddenly as it had started, the noise stopped. And across the street, a light went on in the Parsons' bedroom window. Time for Mrs. Janelle Parson to wake up so she could get to her job at the bakery.

Heavenly's mouth dropped open. How had she heard Mrs. Parson's alarm clock? She shook her head and tried to go back to sleep. She had just drifted off when another alarm woke her, an insistent buzzing that sounded like a swarm of bees. Heavenly looked out her window again. Next door a light came on at the Pearlies' house—and the buzzing stopped.

Before her own alarm went off at six thirty, Heavenly heard thirteen more alarms in houses up and down her street, as well as the whistle from a factory she was pretty sure was located a dozen miles away in Tintown. *Everyone certainly wants to make sure they get up on time,* she thought grumpily as she tried to fall asleep again.

By six thirty Heavenly was lying wide-awake in her bed. When her alarm clanged, she swatted at the little button on top.

Brrrrring! Brrrrrrring!

"Turn *off!*" cried Heavenly.

Brrrrring! Brrrrrring!

"I said, *turn off!*"

The alarm rang continuously. Heavenly hit the button again, but still the ringing wouldn't stop. It sounded like this: *ringringringringringringring ringringringringring-ringringringringringrinringringringringringringringring-ringringringringringringringringringringringringringring-ringringringringring.*

At last Heavenly was dressed and standing in the kitchen. Following Missy's instructions, she was wearing the watch.

"You're on time again," exclaimed her amazed parents, and the ringing stopped.

Heavenly slumped onto her chair and rested her head on the table. "Yup." She frowned at her parents. "Um, how did you sleep?"

"Like logs," said her father.

"Great," said her mother. "Straight through the night. Cramden, too. How did you sleep?"

"Oh, you know," Heavenly answered vaguely.

The Earwigs watched their daughter dawdle through her breakfast. She stirred her spoon around in her cereal and said, "What if there were teeny, tiny boats the size of peas that you could sail in your cereal?"

Mr. Earwig checked his own watch and was just about to tell Heavenly to hurry up or she would miss her bus when his daughter shot to her feet and clapped her hands over her ears.

"I guess it's time for me to go!" she shouted, and she grabbed her backpack and flew out the front door.

Once again Mr. and Mrs. Earwig looked at each other in astonishment.

In school Heavenly heard bells and whistles throughout the day. She heard a ringing sound and saw the kindergarteners rush outside for recess. She heard the factory whistle again and knew the workers were about to go on their lunch break. *Ring, ring, ring, tweet, tweet, tweet* all day long. The world was operating on a schedule.

The alarm on Heavenly's watch had rung—ear shatteringly—each time she was about to be late for something: gym, lunch, and just before Mr. Reading the librarian came to her room to remind her about an overdue book. By the end of the day, Heavenly's head ached. When the final school bell rang, she leaped to her feet, grabbed her backpack, and ran outside directly to her bus. She glared at her watch, but it was silent. Heavenly waited impatiently for Mr. Howard to open the bus door. When he did, she hurried down the aisle and realized she could claim a spot at the very back of the bus, where the seats were the bounciest when going over bumps. At her bus stop, she hopped down the steps and ran straight to her house. Once again she eyed her watch, but it didn't make a sound.

Heavenly realized she hadn't heard any other bells in a while, either. The noise in her head was beginning to settle down.

"You made the bus!" was Mrs. Earwig's greeting when her daughter ran breathlessly into the house. She set a plate of cookies in front of her.

"Homework time," said Mrs. Earwig later, and Heavenly thought her mother winced just slightly.

But Heavenly said, "Okay," and ran upstairs with her books. She looked longingly at her drawings of the twenty-two children, but she set them aside hastily when she heard a vague ringing from somewhere in her room.

Heavenly was five minutes early for dinner that night, and her father said they could make popcorn later as a treat.

At the upside-down house that evening, Missy picked up the phone and dialed Heavenly's number. "How's everything going?" she asked Mrs. Earwig.

"Oh, Missy, you're a marvel! Heavenly was on time for breakfast and dinner, and she didn't miss the bus."

"Wonderful," replied Missy. "I think she can return the watch to me tomorrow."

Missy hung up the phone and turned to Lester, who was sitting on the couch drinking a cup of coffee. "Problem solved," she said, and poured a cup for herself.

7

Honoriah Freeforall, or the Know-It-All Cure

MISSY PIGGLE-WIGGLE FINISHED up her farm chores and looked around the neat barn with satisfaction. "There's nothing like a job well done," she said to Lightfoot, who, for the first time since Missy had arrived in Little Spring Valley, twined about her ankles and purred softly.

Missy reached down to scratch her ears, and then she whistled for Wag. "Come on, boy. Time to go to the Freeforalls'."

Wag came running through the fenced-in yard, ears flying, and Missy held the back door to the upside-down house open for him. "I think," she said, "that today is the day to give Honoriah the Know-It-All Cure."

From the cabinet of cures in her bedroom she selected a slender vial, which she dropped into her satchel. She had just started down the stairs to the first floor when she reached for the banister, realized that it had disappeared, and nearly fell over the edge and into the hallway below.

"Careful! Careful!" squawked Penelope. She flew by Missy in alarm.

Missy flung herself against the wall. "House! Put the banister back immediately!"

The banister reappeared.

"That was incredibly naughty, House," said Missy. "Do not ever do that again, particularly if children are here."

The last part of this admonishment was unnecessary since Missy had already discovered that the house loved children.

The banister stayed in place, and Missy and Wag left the house without further trouble. "You're in charge, Lester!" Missy called as she closed the front door.

It was a lovely, sunny afternoon. Wag trotted jauntily at Missy's heels as they made their way to Juniper Street, Missy's satchel slung invisibly over her shoulder.

"I think we'll just stop in at A to Z Books," Missy said to Wag. She checked her watch. "We have time, and I'd like to chat with Harold for a bit." Missy noticed that when she said Harold's name aloud, the oddest feeling came over her. A pleasant warm feeling, like sunshine. She smiled.

"Harold?" called Missy as she and Wag entered the bookstore and the door sneezed behind them.

Harold hurried out of the storeroom. "What a nice surprise!"

"Just stopping in to say hello." Missy was aware that her cheeks were burning. She paused to glance at herself in a mirror and saw that under her straw hat, her face had turned as red as her hair. Then she turned around and noticed that Harold's face was the same fiery shade.

"Well," said Harold.

"Well," said Missy.

They stared uncomfortably at each other. Finally Harold said, "Read any good books lately?"

"Oh, um, well," stammered Missy. And then she caught herself. It would never do to appear so flustered. "Absolutely," she said firmly. "Absolutely. Melody and I are reading *Chitty Chitty Bang Bang* together. After that we're going to start *Harriet the Spy*."

"Brilliant choices," said Harold.

Missy patted the invisible satchel, clapped her hands together once, and said crisply, "Wag and I must be on our way. It's our afternoon at the Freeforalls'."

Harold had been about to say, "How's that going?" but Missy was already halfway out the door. From the sidewalk, she waved to Harold, and then she and Wag launched themselves down Juniper Street.

"Extraordinary woman," murmured Harold. He stood at the window and gazed after Missy.

~~~~~

Honoriah Freeforall leaned against the kitchen sink, her arms crossed over her chest. "That's not the way *I* would do it!" she exclaimed. She was watching Petulance make chocolate milk. Missy was watching, too.

"That's not the way you would do what?" asked Petulance.

"Make chocolate milk."

Petulance shrugged. "It's how I do it. Why do you care? And anyway, what's wrong with the way I'm doing it?"

"You should have put the chocolate powder in first, not the milk. Now the powder's just floating on top."

Petulance shrugged again.

"Give it to me," said Honoriah, reaching for the glass.

Petulance snatched it away, and milk slopped onto the floor. "Now look what you made me do!"

"It was your fault," said Honoriah.

"Hmm," said Missy, and she reached into her satchel.

Honoriah and Petulance stared in fascination as a small glass vial appeared in Missy's hand.

"You must feel awfully frustrated, Honoriah," Missy said, "when people don't take your suggestions."

"Oh, I *do*. No one ever listens to me."

"Perhaps a bit of magic is called for."

Honoriah's eyes grew wide. "Your magic?"

"Who else's?"

Honoriah frowned. "What will the magic do?" After a moment she added, "I don't have to swallow a potion, do I?"

Frankfort, who had been watching from the table where his homework was spread in front of him, said, "Of course you do. And it's made from your own ground-up toenails."

"Missy!" cried Honoriah.

"The cure," Missy said calmly, "is just a vapor that will waft around you. You don't have to drink a potion."

"See?" said Honoriah, and she stuck her tongue out at Frankfort. "You don't know anything."

"Whatever."

Missy uncorked the bottle. A cloud of pink seeped out and wound its way toward Honoriah. It twined around her until she was enveloped in a pale fog.

"It smells like roses," whispered Honoriah.

The vapor became wisps that trailed away to nothing.

"Now what?" Petulance asked Missy.

"Wait and see."

The twins joined Frankfort at the table. Petulance

pulled out her science book and got to work. Honoriah leaned over and peered at her brother's project. "What's that?" she asked.

"We're supposed to make a collage about birds in our region."

"A collage?" said Honoriah. "But that's not how you make a collage."

"It isn't?" exclaimed Frankfort. "What am I doing wrong?"

Honoriah looked surprised but said, "You're just drawing pictures of birds. You're supposed to go through magazines and catalogs and cut out photos and arrange them artistically to make a statement."

"Really? Gosh, I guess I don't know *anything* about collages. What kind of pictures am I looking for?"

"Pictures of *birds*," said Honoriah. "Or birdhouses or wings or beaks."

Frankfort gazed helplessly at his sister. "What if I don't find the right pictures?"

"I don't think there's any right or wrong with a collage," said Honoriah, turning to her own homework.

Frankfort retrieved a magazine from the recycling

bin. He paged through it. "Is this a good picture?" he asked his sister. "Is this? How about this one?"

"They're all good."

"Well, how do I arrange them?"

"Frankfort, I can't do your work for you."

"But you're an expert."

Honoriah's cheeks turned faintly pink, the color of the magic vapor. "I guess that's true," she said, and took the scissors from Frankfort's outstretched hand.

When homework time was over at last—and it took a lot longer than usual since Petulance and Frankfort seemed to need an awful lot of help from Honoriah— Petulance said, "Let's go play on our scooters. Missy, can Wag come with us? I want to give him a ride."

"You can't take Wag on a scooter!" exclaimed Honoriah. "Besides, you don't ride your scooter the right way."

"I *don't?*" said Petulance. "What do I do wrong?"

"Everything."

"Will you show me the right way?"

"Can you give us lessons?" asked Frankfort. "I'd like a scooter lesson."

"Yeah, give us lessons," said Petulance.

Missy watched the Freeforall children disappear out the door, a smile on her face.

By the end of the day, Honoriah found that she was rather tired. She had finished Frankfort's collage for him, given scooter lessons, shown Frankfort the proper way to make a peanut-butter sandwich, and answered about a thousand questions. It seemed that every two seconds, either Frankfort or Petulance was at her bedroom door, looking confused and helpless.

Petulance held out her knitting. "I dropped a stitch! Can you show me how to pick it up?"

Frankfort held out a necktie. "How do you tie this?"

Petulance held out her science book. "What are your tips for memorizing?"

Frankfort held out a pad of paper. "I want to make a card for Missy. How do you draw a dog?"

Honoriah overslept the next morning. Her head hurt and her eyes ached. She'd had a long dream about giving piano lessons to Peony LaCarte. Peony kept saying, "Show me how to play 'Chopsticks,'" and Honoriah had played the song for her 112 times.

Honoriah nearly fell asleep in school. Her eyelids

drooped, and she woke up only when Humphrey Baton tripped over her foot and fell down in the aisle.

"Goodness, Humphrey," said Mrs. Justice, rushing to his side. "Are you all right?"

"I banged my knee." Humphrey sounded tearful.

"You should get him some ice," said Honoriah. "That's what you do for a bump."

"Good thinking," said Mrs. Justice. "Why don't you run to the nurse's office and get an ice pack for Humphrey?"

Honoriah sighed and set off through the hallways. She didn't want to go to the nurse's office. Often, someone in there was bleeding. When she reached the office, she closed her eyes and asked Mrs. Pazden for an ice pack for Humphrey.

"Why are your eyes closed?" said a small voice from the bench by the door.

Honoriah opened her eyes to find out who had spoken and saw a kindergartener with a horribly bloody knee. She clapped her hands over her eyes and kept them there until Mrs. Pazden had handed her the ice pack. She hurried it back to Mrs. Justice.

That afternoon, which was not a Tuesday or a

Thursday, turned out to be one of those afternoons when half the children in Little Spring Valley gathered at Missy's. The day was rainy, and the children were all crammed indoors.

"What a crowd! What a crowd!" Penelope screeched.

Lightfoot arched her back and swatted at passing feet.

Wag ran from room to room, leaping on furniture.

In the kitchen, where four children were eating spaghetti, Lester politely passed around napkins.

Melody Flowers peeked into the dining room and found Heavenly Earwig and Honoriah and Petulance Freeforall sitting cross-legged on top of the table (Missy never seemed to mind if they didn't use chairs), hunched over a large piece of paper. Melody watched them for a few moments.

"Want to help us?" asked Heavenly.

"What are you doing?" Melody remained planted in the doorway.

"Inventing a game," Honoriah replied.

"What kind of game?"

"A board game."

"But what's it about?"

"We don't know yet," said Petulance. "We're still deciding."

"Maybe it should be about cats," said Heavenly.

Honoriah wrinkled her nose.

"Baseball," suggested Petulance.

"How about a game about the people of Little Spring Valley?" said Melody, and the other girls turned to look at her.

"That's perfect!" exclaimed Honoriah.

Melody edged into the room and climbed onto the table.

"The object of the game," Heavenly said, "will be to go all the way around the board and get home on time."

"Really?" said Honoriah. "That's kind of boring."

"Well, I don't know anything about making a game," said Heavenly.

"Yeah, how do you make a game?" asked Petulance.

"Maybe you start with rules," Heavenly replied.

Petulance looked thoughtful. "Okay, how about: Rule number one—if you roll double sixes, you get a free turn?"

"A free turn to do what?" said Honoriah. "You have

to decide the *object* of the game first. *Then* you make up the rules."

"The object is traveling around town and getting home on time," Heavenly insisted.

"No, that's no good," said Honoriah.

"Then *you* make up the game," said Heavenly. "We'll do something else while we wait."

Melody handed Honoriah a pen, and Honoriah began writing down rules and drawing a game board. Heavenly, Petulance, and Melody decided to give Wag a makeover.

"You just keep working on the game," Petulance called to her sister as she tied ribbons around Wag's ears.

"Yeah, call us when it's ready," added Heavenly. "Hey, Melody, do you want to come over to my house tomorrow? We could give my brother a makeover."

It took Honoriah, working all by herself, nearly two hours to invent a game called Trouble at the LaCartes'. "Finished!" she called, just as Petulance stuck her head into the dining room and said, "It's dinnertime. We have to go home now."

"But—but—" stammered Honoriah. "I worked all afternoon on this."

"Take it home with you," suggested Missy. "You and Petulance and Frankfort can play it tonight."

"No," said Honoriah dully. "It's a game for eight people. I'll leave it here."

~~~~~

On Saturday Mr. Hudson Freeforall sat before the computer in his home office. In the room next door, his wife sat at her computer. Through the window he could hear faint sounds from Frankfort and the twins. They had been very quiet for over an hour. Mr. Freeforall began to feel nervous, and he peeked outside.

A rickety wooden structure had appeared in the fork of an oak tree. Honoriah, wearing a pair of overalls, was standing under the structure holding a can of paint. At her feet were a hammer, a jar of nails, and a pile of scrap lumber. Petulance and Frankfort were reclining on lawn chairs, looking at her.

Hesitantly, Mr. Freeforall raised the window. "What's going on out there?" he asked.

"We're building a tree fort," said Frankfort.

"It looks like Honoriah's doing all the work."

"Well, that's because I said, 'Let's build a tree fort,' and Honoriah said, 'Okay,' and I said, 'It should be four feet off the ground,' and Honoriah said, 'How about six?' and I said, 'I guess I don't know a single thing about building forts.'"

Petulance got to her feet. "And then *I* said, 'The fort should have three windows and one door,' and Honoriah said, 'Don't you think too much rain will get in?' and I said, 'Why don't you just go ahead and build the whole fort since we're clueless?' So that's what's happening."

"Tell us again how you make the windows," Frankfort said to his sister.

Honoriah set down the can of paint. Then she sat on it, her chin in her hands. She yawned. "I suppose you have to saw pieces of wood into different lengths."

"What lengths exactly?" asked Petulance.

Honoriah glanced at a measuring tape. "Well—"

"Will the door be able to open and close?" Frankfort interrupted.

"I'm not sure yet. Do you want the door to open and close?"

Frankfort looked at Petulance. He opened his mouth and closed it. Then he opened it again. No sound came out.

Mr. Freeforall watched his children with interest. Petulance seemed to be speechless, too. He was glad his children weren't arguing, but he felt that Honoriah looked tired and a bit pale. And nobody seemed to be having much fun.

He poked his head into his wife's office. "Dear," he said, "when did Missy give Honoriah the Know-It-All Cure?"

"Last week sometime, I think."

"I have a feeling it's worked."

"Really?" replied Mrs. Freeforall. "That Missy is a genius."

"Doesn't she have to reverse her spell, or whatever it is she's done?"

"Hmm? Oh. I don't know. Why don't you call her?"

Mr. Freeforall phoned the upside-down house and explained the situation.

"No arguing?" asked Missy.

"Not a single cross word. But Honoriah's doing all the work, and the others are just watching."

"Why don't you send Honoriah over here?" suggested Missy. "I'll take care of things."

~~~~~

Honoriah made her way to Missy's. She waved to two boys who were digging a hole in the front lawn and said hello to Harold Spectacle, who was sitting on the front porch filling up water balloons with Melody and Heavenly.

"Come into the kitchen!" Missy called to Honoriah.

Honoriah sat at the table. "Everyone listens to me too much now," she said.

"Do you listen to them?" asked Missy. She was patting all the pockets of her dress, searching for something.

"Yes," said Honoriah solemnly.

Missy brightened. "Ah! Here we are." From a pocket on the very back of her dress, she withdrew the small glass vial that Honoriah had seen before. "Hold still," she said.

Honoriah watched as pink fog seeped out of her skin and hair and gathered itself into a rose-scented ball. The ball hung in the air for a moment, and then with a whoosh, the vial drew it in, like Frankfort slurping up a strand of spaghetti.

"That should do it," said Missy. "Would you like some lemonade?"

Honoriah sat on the porch with Harold and Missy and her friends and drank lemonade served by Lester the polite pig.

8
The I-Spy Cure

THERE WAS TROUBLE at the Goodenoughs' house. Everyone in Little Spring Valley agreed about that. And they were very grateful that this particular kind of trouble hadn't affected their own families.

"It's Rusty," the grown-ups whispered to one another at the supermarket.

"Spying," they said as they sipped coffee and watched their children's early morning soccer games. "Eavesdropping."

Even Rusty's teachers noticed. "I'm glad he's not in my class," Mr. Bovine said to Mrs. Justice.

"Try being his sister," Tulip said to Melody as they walked to school one day.

Melody didn't have a brother (or a sister) but had always thought she would like one. "He spies on you?" she said.

"All the time. He's getting ready for a career in espionage."

Rusty was quite a nice boy apart from his unwelcome dedication to espionage. He was polite to his teachers. He brought home report cards with mostly As and only a few Bs and Cs, and once a D. He did his chores without being prodded. He didn't interrupt, even when adults were telling boring, meaningless stories about their childhoods. He could make sad people laugh and lonely children feel that they belonged. He always volunteered to show new students around school.

But he spied. He wanted to hone his skills early to one day get the best possible job in the spy trade.

"He spies through keyholes and underneath doors," Mr. Goodenough told his next-door neighbor, Mr. Potter. "It's like his eyes are everywhere."

Mr. Potter's face grew red. "Last weekend I snuck

out to our garden shed to eat a cupcake. Harriet and I have been on a diet for two weeks. That was the first time I cheated, and Rusty caught me. I looked at the window of the shed, and I could just see his hair and the very tops of his eyes. Then he slowly ducked down."

Mr. Goodenough shoved his hands into his pockets. "I'm sorry," he said. Then he added, "I think he has a periscope, in order to see around corners and above his head."

"How annoying."

At Melody's house one afternoon, Tulip exclaimed, "He knows everything about me! Things that are supposed to be secret."

Melody hadn't known Tulip long enough to ask what her secrets were. Instead she said, "How does he find out your secrets?"

"He listens at doors, he eavesdrops on my phone conversations, and he spies. He's always spying! He's good at it, too. He has a periscope, like a movie spy. Once I was in the bathroom writing a private note, and I noticed the top of the periscope outside the window. He was down below, balanced on the porch roof.

I opened the window and yelled at him, but he just slid off the roof and ran away."

"Why do you think he wants to know everyone's secrets?" asked Melody.

Tulip rolled her eyes. "For his career. But it's not right! He's found out all sorts of things. He saw me borrowing Mom's diamond earrings. Well, not borrowing, I guess, since she had told me I wasn't allowed to wear them. And he saw me sneak a sip of my father's coffee. And he overheard me on the phone telling Honoriah that Mrs. Potter is cheating on her diet. That wasn't so bad, but I had told Honoriah *in private.* If I'd wanted Rusty to know, I would have told him myself."

"You don't keep a diary, do you?" asked Melody.

"Oh no," said Tulip, and she put her head in her hands.

~~~~~

One Saturday, just after school ended for the summer, Mrs. Goodenough returned from the supermarket with a carload of groceries. She pulled into the driveway and approached the garage, her mind on the dinner party she and her husband were giving that night.

She wasn't sure she'd bought enough lettuce for the salad. "Maybe I should turn around and go back right now for another head," she said aloud. But in almost the same instant, she remembered that Harriet Potter detested vegetables, which was probably why she needed to be on a diet in the first place, so she decided she had enough lettuce after all.

"That's settled!" she exclaimed, but in her distraction her hands slipped from the steering wheel, and she ran into the side of the garage.

Mrs. Goodenough screeched the car to a halt. She closed her eyes. Then she opened them, got out of the car, and inspected the damage. A long scrape ran from the back door to the rear bumper. Slowly, she carried the grocery bags into the kitchen. As she unpacked the food, she began to weave a tale. She would tell her family that she had been in town buying the party supplies, just minding her own business, when out of nowhere a garbage truck had come barreling down Juniper Street and sideswiped her car. She had tried to read the license plate on the truck but couldn't because it was covered with garbage, and before she knew it, the truck was out of sight.

At that moment her husband entered the kitchen. "Dear," Mrs. Goodenough began.

"Hey, Dad!" cried Rusty, rushing through the doorway. "Did you see what Mom did to the car?"

"What?" said Mr. Goodenough.

"*What?*" said Mrs. Goodenough.

"You're going to have to have it repainted!" exclaimed Rusty.

"Have what repainted?" asked his father.

His mother sank into a chair. "The side of the car," she admitted.

"And the side of the garage," said Rusty. "There's white garage paint on the car, and green car paint on the garage."

Mr. Goodenough looked from his wife to his son. "What?" he said again.

"I had a little mishap with the car," replied Mrs. Goodenough. She turned her gaze on Rusty. "How do you know what happened?" she asked.

"I was in the bushes by the driveway," he began.

"Why were you in the bushes?" asked his father.

Rusty hesitated. "Well . . . I was hoping to follow Mr. Potter when he left his house. I think he's—"

Mr. Goodenough held up his hands. "Rusty, stop. You can't spy on people and pry into their personal business."

"But their personal business is very interesting to me. Anyway, don't you want to know what happened to the car?"

"Rusty, *I* was going to tell your father what happened," said Mrs. Goodenough. She didn't feel she needed to add that she'd been planning to tell a big fat lie.

Mr. Goodenough suddenly noticed that Rusty was standing in the kitchen with his hands behind his back. "Are you hiding something?" he asked.

Rusty held out one hand, put it behind his back, and then held out the other hand. Each was empty. "Nope," he said.

"Please show me both of your hands at the same time," said his father.

Rusty did so. The periscope clunked to the floor. His father grabbed it. "Go to your room," he said.

"Can I have my periscope?"

"No."

"Mom?"

"No."

"This is so unfair!" Rusty exploded. "This is the most unfair thing you've ever done to me. In my whole life. Why do you want me to be miserable? I'll probably grow up to be a criminal now."

"We don't want you to be miserable. And we're trying to *prevent* you from becoming a criminal," said Mrs. Goodenough.

"You need to respect people's privacy," added Mr. Goodenough. "Your family and your neighbors are *not* the bad guys."

"Well, you need to respect my *property!*" exclaimed Rusty. "You're periscope stealers." He stomped upstairs to his room. With every step, the staircase shook. He slammed his door. Then he opened it again. "Tulip borrowed Mom's diamond earrings!" he yelled. His door slammed a second time.

The Goodenoughs sat across from each other at the kitchen table. "My," said Rusty's mother. "He doesn't usually get upset. What's happened to our nice, polite child?"

"I don't know, but the spying has got to stop."

"It's out of control," agreed Mrs. Goodenough.

"I'll bet the LaCartes never have to deal with this sort of thing."

Throughout Little Spring Valley, the LaCarte children were held up as examples of sterling behavior.

"I wonder if the Potter kids played spy games when they were young. Maybe I could ask Harriet for advice," said Mrs. Goodenough.

"Perhaps over dinner tonight," said her husband.

Mrs. Goodenough frowned. "I don't think so. The LaCartes will be here. I'd rather not discuss Rusty in front of them."

Her husband drummed his fingers on the table. "There's always Missy Piggle-Wiggle."

"That's true." His wife brightened. "I'll call her right now. This is practically an emergency."

When the phone rang in the upside-down house, Penelope screeched, "Telephone! Telephone!" and Lester picked up the receiver and handed it to Missy.

"Thank you," said Missy, who was being given a makeover by Petulance and Heavenly. Heavenly was

braiding Missy's long red hair, and Petulance was paint-
ing her nails. Missy took the phone gingerly. "Hello?"
she said, and blew on her nails.

"Oh, Missy!" cried the voice on the other end. "We
have a terrible problem." There was a gulp and a sort of
a hiccup, and then the voice said, "This is Mrs. Goodenough."

"Ah," said Missy. "I expect you're calling about the
spying."

"Yes. It's—it's—"

"Out of control, no doubt."

Another hiccup. "Yes."

"Could you come over in an hour?"

"Of course. Thank you."

Mrs. Goodenough didn't want to wait an hour, but
she had no choice. She washed lettuce for the salad
and checked her watch again and again until it was
time to leave. She hadn't been to the Piggle-Wiggle
house before: An upside-down house with a magical
little woman in it who could cure children of all their
annoying habits and problems. She found that she felt
rather nervous.

Rusty's mother stood uncertainly on the front porch of the funny brown house with its roof in the ground and rang the bell. She jumped when Penelope hollered, "Missy, Helene Goodenough is here!"

The door was answered by Missy herself, wearing a straw hat, a long braid draped over her shoulder. Her nails had been painted a bright, bright sparkling green. She held a small tin box toward Mrs. Goodenough. "I'm sorry you're having problems with Rusty," she said. "Spying can get to be quite troublesome, and it's hard on the entire family."

"Everyone in *town* knows about it," said Mrs. Goodenough.

"Well, these should do the trick."

Rusty's mother looked at the box. "Licorice drops?" she said. She had heard that Missy's cures were unusual, but . . . candy?

"Not just any licorice drops," Missy replied. "Trust me. All you have to do is give Rusty two today and two tomorrow morning. You should see results almost immediately."

Despite everything that had happened that day,

Mrs. Goodenough felt apprehensive. "Dear," she said to her husband when she returned with the tin box, "we don't even know what these are."

Her husband opened the box. He sniffed the contents. He touched his finger to one of the candies and tasted it. "Licorice."

"I don't think it's just any old licorice."

Mr. Goodenough glanced at the periscope, which was lying on the kitchen counter. "I think we should give it a try. Rusty!" he called.

Rusty came running down the stairs. "Did you decide to give me my periscope back?"

"No, but I have something special for you from Missy Piggle-Wiggle." He held out two of the licorice drops.

Rusty swallowed them and asked once again for the periscope.

"Nope," said his parents.

"Why do you hate me?" shouted Rusty, and clomped up the stairs. On the way to his room, he passed Tulip's door. He could see her seated at her desk, writing something that she was covering with her hand. Rusty continued to his room, whistling, and said loudly, "I think I'll just take a nap now." He closed his door. Then he opened it silently, tiptoed back to Tulip's room, and peeked around the doorway. His sister was still seated at her desk. Rusty leaned in farther and tried to read what she was writing.

That was when Tulip disappeared.

One moment she was seated at her desk, and the next moment she had vanished. Rusty could see her pencil moving across her notebook. He could see her impression on the pillow of her chair. But he couldn't see his sister.

He ducked back into the hall and shook his head. Then he peered into his sister's room again. The pencil was still scratching across the paper. He thought for a moment. "Tulip?" he called.

"Yeah? I thought you were taking a nap."

"Where are you?"

"In my room. And I'm busy. Don't come in here." Her door closed then, apparently by itself.

Rusty retreated to his own room. He spent the rest of the afternoon nervously looking for his sister. He watched Tulip's bicycle wheel itself out of the garage and pedal down the street. He saw the bicycle return shortly before dinner. Over supper, which Rusty and Tulip ate quickly in the kitchen before the party guests arrived, Rusty watched Tulip's fork and spoon move themselves around over her plate. He watched her food disappear. But he didn't see his sister.

"Mom? Dad?" said Rusty. "Do you notice anything, um, unusual about Tulip?"

His parents frowned at each other. "Her clothes are a bit muddy," said his mother after a moment. "Tulip, how did you get so dirty?"

"Playing in the brook with Melody," Tulip's voice replied.

"Okay. Well, change your clothes before the company arrives."

That night, each time the doorbell rang, the guests greeted Rusty and his sister. Rusty watched wide-eyed as the guests shook hands with the air before turning to shake his hand. At last his father said, "Okay, you two. Off to bed."

"Dad, it's summer vacation," said Tulip's voice from

somewhere across the living room. "Can't we stay up for another hour?"

"One hour. Now scoot."

Rusty started up the staircase. He didn't know where Tulip was, and he didn't want to go smashing into her in full view of the guests. Then he heard her rude voice behind him say, "Move it!" and he felt a shove in his back. He ran for his room, where he sat nervously on his bed. *Now* where was his sister? She could be standing right in his doorway, spying on him.

Rusty got up and hastily closed his door.

He sat on his bed again but then realized that Tulip might be peeking at him through the keyhole. He stuck a piece of tape over the hole. Then he stuffed a blanket into the crack below his door. *Then* he realized that Tulip might be *in* his room. How would he know? She could just be standing somewhere, watching him.

Rusty climbed uncomfortably into bed with a book. He read one page. He had the distinct feeling that a pair of eyes was on him. "Tulip?" he called.

No answer.

"Tulip?"

"What?"

"Where are you?"

"In my room. Stop bothering me."

Had Tulip's voice really come from the direction of her room? Rusty glanced toward his window. She could be out on the roof. He pulled the blind down. Then he drew the curtains shut. There. That should do it. No one could see into his room at all.

~~~~~

Now, you would think that after such an unsettling evening, a smart boy like Rusty would know better than to fall into the habit of spying again, even if it meant getting one step closer to an exciting career. But the very next morning, not long after his mother had given him two more licorice drops, Rusty spotted his father carrying a cardboard carton out of the basement, and he decided he just had to know what was in the box. Especially since his father appeared somewhat furtive, glancing from right to left and behind him as he hurried the box through the yard and out to the recycling bins.

Rusty eased the back door open. He tiptoed after his father.

And his father disappeared from sight, vanished into thin air.

Rusty let out a scream, which he tried to stifle.

"Son?" called his father's voice. "Everything okay?"

"Um, yes," croaked Rusty, despite the fact that he had recently discovered that Tulip was still invisible to him. He had crashed into her in the bathroom where, it turned out, she was standing at the sink brushing her teeth. Somehow, he hadn't noticed the floating tooth-brush.

"What is *wrong* with you?" she'd exclaimed, tooth-paste spraying across Rusty's face.

Rusty had turned and run.

The rest of the day was just as uncomfortable for Rusty as you might imagine. In desperation, he spent the afternoon across town at Georgie Pepperpot's, where he hoped that neither Tulip nor his father was spying on him.

The next morning Rusty ate breakfast with his mother, his sister's voice, and his father's voice, watching forks and knives raise and lower themselves over plates, chairs shove themselves under the table, and flying toast disappear bite by bite. As soon as the meal was over, he hurled himself into the garage, climbed on his bicycle, and rode around and around town, occasionally calling out, "Tulip?" She never answered, and Rusty saw no riderless bicycles, but he wondered if she was still running after him, spying on him, hoping to learn a secret or two, although as far as Rusty knew, she didn't plan on a career in espionage.

"I'll show her," Rusty finally said. He threw down his bicycle and sat on a bench on Juniper Street. "I'll be the most boring person ever. No one will *want* to spy on me."

At that moment he heard the door of A to Z Books sneeze, and who should come out of the store but Missy and Harold.

"Huh," thought Rusty. "I wonder where they're going."

He stood up to follow them but realized just in time what would happen if he did, and he squeezed his eyes shut.

"Rusty?" said a voice. He thought it belonged to Missy.

Heart pounding, Rusty opened his eyes. He let out a sigh of relief. Missy and Harold were standing in front of him.

"Are you all right?" asked Missy.

Rusty thought about the question. "Not really. Could I talk to you?" Then he added, "In private?"

Harold smiled at him. "I have things to do in town," he said, and walked away.

That afternoon Rusty and Missy had a long talk at the upside-down house. They sat on the porch, and Lester served them lemonade.

"I have to tell you something," Rusty began. He knew he could tell Missy Piggle-Wiggle anything in the world, and she would understand. But suddenly he couldn't find the words he wanted.

"Is it about spying?" asked Missy.

Rusty nodded. "Yes." And then he told her about Tulip and his father and the past couple of days. "I never knew if Tulip was watching me. It's been horrible."

"It's uncomfortable to imagine that someone is

spying on you," agreed Missy. "Watching you when you think you're alone. Learning your secrets."

"It wasn't really about secrets," Rusty replied. "I don't have any. But it was—"

"An invasion of your privacy?"

Rusty nodded again.

"I think," said Missy after a moment, "that you'll be able to keep your eyes and ears to yourself from now on. What do you think?"

"I can do that. But it won't be easy. I like to know things. Uncovering mysteries is how I practice for my spy career."

"Maybe sometimes a little bit of mystery is good."

"That's true," said Rusty, who very much enjoyed all the mysteries at the upside-down house and realized that he would rather not know if there was truly any pirate treasure buried in the yard. It was much more fun to dig and hope.

He said so to Missy.

Missy smiled and thought about the licorice drops.

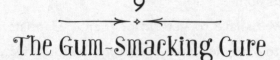

9
The Gum-Smacking Cure

HANNAFORD AND MARIELLE Pettigrew took parenting very seriously. They had one child—Linden—and they bought book after book about raising a healthy child in the twenty-first century. For the first few years of his life, they managed to keep Linden away from junk food, television, action figures, and other bad influences. They gave him organic sugar-free low-fat yogurt and called it ice cream. Whenever they passed the toy store at the end of Juniper Street, they told him it was actually a toy museum and that anyway it was closed.

Television presented a slightly larger problem. Hannaford and Marielle liked television quite a bit, and when Linden was born, they had three flat-screen TVs in their home.

"We'll have to get rid of them," Hannaford said sadly to Marielle on the day they brought Linden home from the hospital.

"Are you sure?" Marielle replied.

Hannaford nodded, the TV sets were given away, and Linden was raised on books and classical music.

Now, it was true that Linden grew up to be a busy and creative boy. He was forever making skyscrapers out of Popsicle sticks and starting collections of things such as stamps and leaves. (He organized the leaves into a herbarium, which he put on display in his living room and for which he charged fifty cents per viewing.) But early on, his parents realized that it was impossible to keep him away from the things, such as television, that all his friends had. One day when he and his mother were walking by the toy museum, Linden paused to look in the window and said, "Ooh, Mommy! There's Superman!"

That night Marielle Pettigrew said to her husband, "How does Linden know who Superman is?"

Hannaford sighed. "Probably from watching television over at the Freeforalls'."

Bit by bit, things fell apart. When Linden was invited to his first slumber party, he watched a movie called *Paul Blart: Mall Cop* and four hours of cartoons. At his friends' houses he played computer games, listened to rap music, and learned how to text. But . . .

Linden did not learn to like junk food. When his friends ate cookies, he asked for free-range chicken nuggets. When they ate ice cream, he ate yogurt. (He didn't mind—much—that his parents had bent the truth about ice cream.) And at his own eighth birthday party, he insisted on serving tuna fish on gluten-free bagels with a fruit salad.

"What do you want to put in your friends' goody bags?" Hannaford asked him when they were planning the party.

Linden thought for a moment. "Banana chips and multigrain crackers."

His parents glanced at each other. "Maybe we could

make just one exception," said Marielle Pettigrew. "For your friends. How about M&M's and Tootsie Pops?"

"Well," said Linden. "All right. As long as I don't have to eat them."

Marielle and Hannaford gave a sigh of relief. Their son was going to be healthy and strong and have a mouth full of beautiful, cavity-free teeth.

The day the invitation to Beaufort Crumpet's birthday party arrived was like any other. Linden went off to day camp with his bag lunch of unsalted cashews, tofu squares, and a package of kale chips. His parents went to work. When they all returned at the end of the day, they looked through the mail.

"Linden, here's something for you," said his mother. She handed him an envelope.

"It's from Beaufort," said Linden. He opened the envelope with a butter knife. "It's an invitation. To a pizza birthday party. You'd better pack some food for me. Beaufort will probably serve cake and ice cream, too."

On the day of the party, Hannaford Pettigrew drove Linden to the mall where Beaufort and his guests were going to have a gymnastics lesson and then eat pizza. Linden carried a present wrapped in bright polka-dotted paper and a bag containing an almond-butter sandwich and some cubed mango. Beaufort and his guests walked on the balance beam, jumped over the horse, and learned how to turn cartwheels. Then, sweaty and hungry, they sat around a big table where pizza was served. Linden ate his sandwich and mango. At the end of the party, when the parents were arriving, Beaufort handed each of his guests a striped goody bag.

Linden waited until he was in the car before he opened the bag and exclaimed in dismay, "Ew! Look, Mom. Lollipops, gummy bears, SweeTARTS. This is disgusting. Well, here's some sugarless gum. Maybe that's not so bad."

Linden peeled back the paper from a stick of gum.

He sniffed it. "Peppermint," he said. "I think."

He licked it. "Interesting."

He bit off a corner and chewed it tentatively. "Hmm. I sort of like this."

Linden put the rest of the stick in his mouth. "Wow. It's like a burst of peppermint on my tongue."

He chewed more enthusiastically. *Chew, chew, chew. Chaw, chaw, chaw.*

The flavor began to fade faster than he had anticipated, so he unpeeled another stick of gum.

"What are you doing?" asked his mother.

"The flavor's already gone. And it was really good."

"All right," said Marielle unhappily.

They reached their house, and the car had barely come to a stop when Linden unfastened his seat belt and flung his door open. He held the goody bag in front of him like a trophy. "Dad! Dad! Look what I got!"

Mr. Pettigrew was sitting on the front porch enjoying a nice glass of iced mint tea without sugar. The day was warm, but the breeze on the porch was cool, and it was that time of afternoon when a summer day begins to creep toward evening and the light fades just enough to remind you that night is returning.

Linden ran to his father, leaned in to his face, and smacked the mouthful of gum. "Peppermint!" he exclaimed.

His father drew back. "You're chewing gum?" He tried to hide his alarm.

"Yep." Linden sat on the floor of the porch and dumped out the goody bag. He brushed away all the candy and even the book of temporary tattoos and the set of fake teeth that would make him look like a vampire. Left in front of him were two more packs of sugarless gum, several pieces of bubble gum, and two gum balls the size of plums. Linden spent the remainder of the afternoon tasting the gum and experimenting with it.

"How do you blow bubbles?" he asked his mother as he unwrapped the first piece of bubble gum, which was a shocking pink color, not sugar-free, and much sweeter than he could have imagined.

His mother refused to look up from the book she was reading. "I don't know," she said, even though she knew perfectly well and as a child had been a champion bubble blower.

"I'll find out online," replied Linden. He sat in front of the Pettigrew family computer, which Linden had convinced his parents he needed in order to do his homework. Within an hour he was blowing bubbles almost as large as his own head. But they kept bursting and getting in his eyes and nose and hair. Linden was undeterred.

"Wow, did you see that? Did you see that?" he asked his parents over and over again.

He bit a hunk out of one of the giant gum balls and chewed away on it for a while. When it began to lose its flavor, he crammed the rest of the gum ball in his mouth.

"Dahmug salvib flittfermip?" he said to his father.

Hannaford, who had moved inside and was starting to prepare dinner in the kitchen, looked up and frowned. "What?"

Linden tried again. "Imfrabagslsh."

"I'm afraid you're impossible to understand." His father said this with a hint of victory, thinking that surely his son would stop chewing gum if no one could understand what he was saying.

But Linden shrugged his shoulders, said, "Shpeshiwog," and went upstairs, still smacking and chewing.

At dinnertime Linden set a saucer by his plate. His parents watched as he removed a giant slobbery wad of gum from his mouth and set it on the saucer.

"Linden, that is disgusting," said Marielle, who was usually careful not to say anything to her son that might wound his feelings or lower his self-esteem.

"How did you even fit that in your mouth?" asked Hannaford.

Linden shrugged again. "Is it okay to leave it on the saucer?" he asked politely. "I thought that would be better than sticking it to the table."

His mother grew pale. "Perhaps you could put the saucer in the kitchen where we can't see it," she said.

"Or outside," muttered his father.

Linden removed the saucer and returned to the dining room. When he and his parents had finished their dinner of salmon and Brussels sprouts, he asked, "Anything for dessert?"

Mr. and Mrs. Pettigrew gasped.

"No, huh?" said Linden. "Okay, I'll just finish my gum."

He went upstairs to his room, where he gnawed and mashed away until no more fresh gum was left. He sat back on his heels, disappointed. He had not perfected his bubble blowing yet.

Linden thought for a moment before rooting around in his closet for the box labeled POPSICLE STICKS AND GLUE. He opened it, removed a layer of Popsicle sticks, and found the hidden bag containing his allowance. He dumped out the coins and bills and counted them.

"Excellent," he said.

~~~~~

The next morning Linden waited impatiently until it was nine o'clock. Day camp was over for the season, and the day stretched ahead of him. Promptly at nine, he hopped on his bicycle and rode to Juniper Street. Ordinarily, he might have left his bike in the rack in front of the library and then walked slowly up and down the street, looking in every window he passed. But this morning Linden rode directly to the Good Ship Lollipop, a store to which he had paid little attention in the past, since it sold nothing but sweets.

Linden jammed his hands in his pockets and stood in front of a shelf full of gum. There was bubble gum, gum that crackled, and sacks of gold-nugget gum. There was gum filled with strawberry liquid, gum balls that looked like baseballs, and a dispenser with six feet of bubble-gum tape.

Linden counted out his money.

And then he spent every last cent on gum.

As you might imagine, Hannaford and Marielle Pettigrew were concerned when Linden came home with four pounds of chewing gum but felt they could say little to him since he had proudly spent his own money on it. All the rest of that day, he chewed and blew bubbles and smacked and smacked and smacked.

He grew increasingly hard to understand.

"Mowmphshlerp," he said to his mother just before dinner.

"I can't understand you," she replied.

Linden withdrew a lump of slimy pinkish-gray gum from his mouth. "I'm not hungry," he told her.

"Well, I'm not surprised, with all the sugar that's in your body."

"I think I'll skip supper," he said before popping the gum back in his mouth.

After dinner, Marielle and Hannaford sat outside on the porch with cups of nice, calming tea.

"What's that noise?" asked Marielle after a moment. She looked above her, toward her son's bedroom windows.

Hannaford listened. "I think it's Linden."

"Smacking his gum?"

"I'm afraid so."

"We have to do something," said Marielle. "That wad of gum is getting bigger by the minute. I can barely understand a word he says. And he doesn't seem to care."

"He's going to get cavities," added Hannaford. "He'll ruin his perfect dental record. What are we going to do?"

"I've heard wonderful things about Missy Piggle-Wiggle."

"Who?"

"Missy Piggle-Wiggle. That funny little magical woman who's Mrs. Piggle-Wiggle's great-niece."

"I thought Mrs. Piggle-Wiggle was the funny little magical woman."

"They both are," Marielle replied. "Did you hear what Missy did for the Earwigs? She cured Heavenly of being tardy."

"I wonder if the LaCartes could recommend her."

"I doubt it. They've probably never needed her. Della and Peony are perfect specimens. I'm going to phone Missy right now."

Marielle went inside and called Missy. When she returned to the porch, she said, "Missy wants Linden to come over first thing tomorrow morning. I wonder what she's going to do."

~~~~~

Linden felt slightly nervous as he walked to the upside-down house the next day. He had played there many times, but never before had he been *sent* there. His mother had looked rather stern when she'd said that Missy was expecting him. Linden dragged his feet all the way, but when he finally arrived, Missy met him at the door holding the most beautiful gum ball he'd ever seen.

"Wow," Linden whispered. "It looks like a globe."

"It's for you," said Missy.

Linden drew in his breath. "There was nothing like this at the Good Ship Lollipop."

"Of course not. This is one of a kind."

Linden turned the gum ball around and around in his hands. "Hey!" he exclaimed. He squinted at it. "Now it looks like an apple." He stared some more. "And now a flower."

"Taste it," said Missy.

Linden stuck out his tongue and licked it. Then he bit into it. "Apple cinnamon!" he exclaimed. His eyes widened. "Wait. Now it tastes like grape. How did it do that?" He didn't wait for an answer. He stuffed the rest of the gum ball in his mouth. "Annowtshmump."

"What?" said Missy.

Linden removed the gum long enough to say, "And now it tastes like maple." He returned the gum to his mouth.

"Like I said, it's one of a kind."

"Shnollupsmeng!" exclaimed Linden. "Bowntfor-thentup!"

Penelope the parrot flapped onto Missy's shoulder and squawked, "He's awfully hard to—"

Lester appeared and swatted at Penelope. She lowered her voice. "He's awfully hard to understand," she said in a parrot whisper.

"Miffenputh?" Linden wanted to know.

"The gum will last forever," Missy answered promptly. "The flavors constantly change, and they never fade. Oh, and the gum is particularly good for popping, smacking, and blowing bubbles."

"Thraphoo!" called Linden as he left the upside-down house and hurried home.

He passed by Melody's yard.

"Hi, Linden," said Melody.

Linden was smacking his gum so loudly that he couldn't hear her. He tried to say, "What?" which came out, "Whumphh?"

"What?" said Melody.

"Whumphh?" said Linden again.

"*What?*"

"Whumphh?"

When Linden ran through his front door, he had intended to call, "Mom! Mom! Missy gave me gum that changes flavor."

Instead he said, "Mmmmummmm," and discovered that his mouth was stuck together. He had to pry his teeth apart with his fingers and pull the gum out.

"What on earth?" exclaimed his mother.

"I have new gum," said Linden, feeling slightly less enthusiastic. He put it back in his mouth.

His mother watched as a strange look crossed his face. "What is it? What's wrong? Linden? Can you hear me?"

Linden couldn't, in fact, hear her over his chewing and smacking. But the real problem was the current flavor of the gum. He hastily removed the wad from his mouth. It sat wetly in his hand.

"What's wrong?" said his mother again. She put her hand on Linden's forehead.

"Um," said Linden, "what's the name of that herb I don't like?"

"Cilantro?"

Linden coughed. "Yeah. Just for a moment the gum tasted like cilantro." Cautiously, he put it back in his mouth and chewed. "Ownirapbry!" he exclaimed, which meant, "Oh, now it's raspberry!"

"What?" said his mother.

"Whumphh?"

Linden went upstairs to his room, where he spent the greater part of the day blowing bubbles, chewing, and trying to identify each flavor of his gum.

Occasionally his teeth stuck together and he had to pry them apart again. But mostly he popped and smacked and practiced his bubble blowing.

"This is horrible," Hannaford said to Marielle that evening. "He's worse than before. I think we should call Missy again."

"But her cures are supposed to work wonders. Let's give it one more day."

"All right," said Hannaford as the scent of popcorn drifted to his nostrils and he realized he was smelling Linden's gum from several rooms away.

In his bedroom, Linden was carefully keeping a list of all the flavors he tasted. He spat out the gum when he tasted cilantro for a second time. He looked down his list. Among all the lovely fruity and sweet flavors, he had also identified anchovy and something that tasted the way dog food smelled. Thankfully the unappealing flavors never lasted long. Linden replaced the gum and managed to make his loudest pop ever.

It sort of hurt his ears.

The next morning Linden slid into his place at the breakfast table, smacked his gum, looked at his parents, and said, "Whumphh?" because he could see that they were talking to him.

He realized his stomach felt queasy. The gum was sour. Not sour in the way gum tastes when the flavor is fading, but sour in a wild, bold way, as if he were chewing on a dirty sponge. He hastily removed the gum. He planned to wait a few seconds before putting it back in his mouth, but he had realized that now even when he was tasting mint or cherry or chocolate pudding, it was harder and harder to un-taste the revolting flavors.

"I'll just put this back up in my room where you don't have to see it," Linden said. He ran upstairs. He set the gum in a dish on his dresser. Then he hesitated. Experimentally, he put the gum back in his mouth. Immediately he spat it out. He sniffed it. "I knew it!" he cried. "Laundry detergent."

"Linden?" called Hannaford from downstairs. His voice sounded awfully loud.

"Coming." Linden walked slowly to the kitchen.

"We'd like to talk with you," said Marielle as he took his place again.

"Okay."

"We've tried not to say anything," his father spoke up.

"About the gum," his mother continued.

Linden felt his face turn pale. His stomach churned. "That's okay," he interrupted. "You don't have to say anything. In fact, *please* don't say anything. Don't ever mention gum again." He thought about the sour sponge and the anchovies and the laundry detergent. "Really. I'd rather not think about it." He burped. "Do we have any chamomile tea?"

10

Frankfort Freeforall, or the Whatever Cure

MISSY PIGGLE-WIGGLE SAT in the rocking chair on her front porch and ruminated, which is an unnecessarily adult way of saying she was thinking things over. It was a cloudy late summer afternoon. School would be starting again soon. Missy couldn't believe that she had been living at the upside-down house for so long. She also couldn't believe that she hadn't heard from her great-aunt. Months had gone by without a phone call or another letter. Not one single word.

She looked at Lester, who was seated on the porch swing, back feet crossed at the ankles as usual, a cup of coffee held between his front hooves. Wag was curled at Missy's feet, and Penelope was perched on her shoulder, her head drooping as she fell asleep.

Where was Auntie? Missy wondered. Was she on a pirate ship, bargaining for the return of her husband? Her search could have taken her anywhere at all in the world—to the high seas, to a desert island, to a jungle or a rain forest, or to someplace entirely ordinary. Although really, when you thought about it, what place was entirely ordinary when Mrs. Piggle-Wiggle was in it?

While Missy was ruminating, Harold Spectacle was walking along in the direction of the upside-down house. He passed Melody playing in her yard with Tulip and Heavenly, and he called to her, "The mystery you ordered is in!"

"Yes!" exclaimed Melody.

Harold smiled but his mind was wandering. He was thinking about Missy Piggle-Wiggle. When he reached the end of the path to the upside-down house and saw Missy sitting on the porch, he could feel his heart begin to pound. He twirled his cane, hoping to appear jaunty and confident. Then he tipped his top hat.

"Good afternoon!" he called.

"Good afternoon to you!"

Harold could think of nothing further to say. For a person who spent his days surrounded by books and words, you might have thought something clever would come to him, but it was as if all his words had vanished.

Missy felt tongue-tied, too, and for a moment wondered if the house was playing a trick. Then Penelope, who was now awake, began bouncing up and down on Missy's shoulder. "Speak up!" she squawked. "Speak up! Somebody say—"

Lester shushed her with a wave of his hoof.

Harold climbed the steps to the porch and leaned on the rail across from Missy.

"Would you like some lemonade?" she asked him, just as he said, "I brought you a book," and then realized he had left it behind at A to Z Books.

"Disaster, disaster," whispered Penelope.

Missy ignored her. She smiled at Harold. "What was the book about?"

"The history of Little Spring Valley. That may not sound very interesting—"

"Oh no, it sounds fascinating. I'd like to know more

about the town. I love history." This wasn't quite true. What Missy loved was magic. But she did want to know more about Little Spring Valley.

"Well, maybe I can take you on a tour of the town sometime," said Harold.

"Thank you," said Missy. "That would be very nice."

After another awkward silence. Harold made a production out of checking his watch, which was a pocket watch that he looked at as if he were an old-time train conductor. "Uh-oh! I must be on my way!" He fled down the path before words could fail him again.

Missy sat back in the rocking chair and tried to relax. She thought about Harold Spectacle and his offer. She thought about Melody. She thought about how the upside-down house was going to be awfully quiet on weekdays once school started.

Then her thoughts turned to Frankfort Freeforall. Like all the children in Little Spring Valley, Frankfort had many good qualities. He was curious and he did well in school. He was an excellent soccer player. He was brave. He was daring. But you couldn't say he was thoughtful or that he was concerned about other people's feelings.

"Whatever!" Frankfort declared about five hundred times a day. It was his response to everything.

"Frankfort, give that back to me. I was playing with it," Linden would exclaim.

"Whatever."

"Frankfort, you just made Melody cry," Tulip would say.

"What. Ever."

"Frankfort, stop chasing Veronica. She's getting tired," Georgie would say.

"What*ever!*"

Sometimes he said "Whatever" just for the fun of it.

"Frankfort—"

"Whatever!"

Frankfort was a problem. Wag hid from him, and so did Veronica and some of the smaller children.

Missy's phone rang. "Hello?" she said.

"Missy?" (Missy recognized Mrs. Freeforall's voice.) "Do you have a moment?"

"Of course."

"I'm sorry to bother you, but I'm sort of at my wits' end with Frankfort and, well, you've worked wonders with the twins."

Missy could see what was coming. She got right to the point. "Frankfort will need a two-step cure for his Whatever-itis."

"Oh dear. It's that bad, is it?"

"Well," Missy began, and paused, thinking about what to say. One had to be diplomatic when discussing people's children. "Not only does Frankfort need to curb his behavior, but he needs to stop hurting and annoying others."

"Absolutely."

"He also needs to think about how others are feeling."

"Mm-hmm."

"In other words, he'll need the Bubble of Apology followed by a How-Are-You-Doing? pill."

In the background Missy heard one of the twins cry, "Ow, Frankfort! That hurt!"

"Whatever!"

"Do you have any questions?" asked Missy.

"How soon can you get started?" said Mrs. Freeforall.

~~~~~

On one of the very last days of summer vacation, Honoriah, Petulance, and Frankfort arrived at the upside-down house early in the morning. Missy knew they'd arrived because she could hear them on the front porch, squabbling over who got to ring the doorbell.

"It's my turn," said Petulance. "We said we would take turns, and today it's my turn."

"Whatever," replied Frankfort.

The next thing Missy knew, Penelope was announcing, "It's the Freeforalls!"

"You're here bright and early," said Missy.

"Mom and Dad are already working," said Honoriah.

"We can't wait for school to start," added Petulance. "Then we'll have something to do instead of waiting for Mom and Dad to do something with us."

The morning was sunny with a breeze that was almost chilly. When Missy looked at the maple tree in the yard, she noticed that the tips of several leaves had turned bright yellow. Fall was on the way. The sun-warmed air seemed to draw the children of Little Spring Valley to the upside-down house that day. By lunchtime, no fewer than seventeen children were climbing through the house and running around the yard and knitting long, red traily things and making papier-mâché masks in the kitchen.

Frankfort had said "Whatever" 362 times.

Missy, her hair springing from under her straw hat, stood at the front door with her hands on her hips and watched him playing hide-and-seek with Georgie, Linden, and Beaufort. Georgie crawled into one of the best hiding places, which was a spot under the front porch, and Frankfort dropped to his hands and knees to follow him.

"Go away!" Georgie hissed. "I was here first."

"Whatever."

"Okeydokey," Missy said to herself. She snapped her fingers, and in the next instant, Frankfort found himself rolling around inside an enormous, glistening bubble.

"Hey!" he shouted. "Help!" The bubble began to drift upward.

Everything in the front yard came to a stop.

Frankfort pounded his hands against the bubble. From down below, he looked like a large hamster in an exercise ball.

The children in the upside-down house dropped their knitting and abandoned their masks. They joined the crowd beneath Frankfort and stared up at him.

"Let me out!" Frankfort yelled. "Let me out! Let me

out!" He punched the inside of the bubble. It was like punching a marshmallow. He kicked. The bubble bobbled and bounced and floated slightly higher as Frankfort tumbled around.

"Wow, that's a really strong bubble," commented Beaufort.

"Let him out," said Linden.

"Let me out!" Frankfort yelled again.

"You can let yourself out," Missy called to him.

"How?"

"Apologize to Georgie."

"No."

Georgie grinned up at him. "Yeah, say you're sorry."

"No."

"Well," said Missy, "I'm going to go inside and make lunch. I think we'll have hot dogs today."

The children took a last look at Frankfort and the bubble and turned toward the house.

"Wait! Wait for me!" Frankfort cried desperately. He ran and ran, pumping his legs against the bubble, which only made him slip and slide and turn somersaults. "I'm sorry, Georgie!" he called. "I'm sorry I was going to take your hiding place."

The bubble floated downward, landed gently in the yard, and disappeared with a soft, damp *pop.*

Frankfort held out his arms and examined them. He looked down at his legs. He patted himself all over. "Huh," he said.

Lunch was a picnic. The children took their plates of hot dogs outside and ate on tablecloths Missy had spread on the ground. Of course Frankfort wanted more than one hot dog, and of course he snatched Veronica's from her plate, and of course Veronica burst into tears and yelped, "That's mine!" and of course Frankfort replied, "Whatever."

I think you know what happened next. Frankfort found himself rolling around inside another bubble. The hot dog was no longer in his hand. It was back on Veronica's plate, and she was staring at it warily. (What you may not have guessed is that Veronica no longer wanted to eat it. "It has boy germs on it," she whispered to Melody.)

Meanwhile, Frankfort, hot dog–less, floated above the picnic. For a while, he tried to pretend that he was having fun up there, rolling around in the air, laughing and hooting as if he were in his own private bouncy castle. But no one paid any attention to him.

Missy began to serve ice cream. Frankfort watched his friends slurp on their cones. Missy produced sprinkles (it looked to Frankfort as if she produced them from the sleeve of her dress), and now the cones seemed to glow in the sunshine.

Frankfort sat in his bubble. *Whatever, whatever, whatever*, he said to himself. He removed a pen from his pocket and jabbed the bubble. Nothing happened.

He pinched the bubble. Nothing.

He scrunched up a great big handful of bubble and gave it a twist. Nothing.

Frankfort stared down at the ice cream party. He thought he could actually smell chocolate ice cream, but that seemed unlikely.

"Frankfort?" Missy called from below.

"What."

"You know how to get out of the bubble, don't you?"

Frankfort stared. "Apologize," he said finally.

"Exactly," said Missy.

Frankfort put his hands to his mouth and shouted, "Veronica, I'm sorry you're such a crybaby."

The bubble swooped higher then, above the top

branches of the maple tree. Frankfort crossed his arms and pretended he wasn't scared. Everyone else probably was, though. He peered down through the limbs of the tree, expecting to see his sisters and friends screaming and jumping up and down. Instead they were helping Missy clean up the picnic. Linden, Beaufort, and Georgie returned to their game.

Whatever, whatever, whatever.

All afternoon Frankfort watched his friends in Missy's yard. The air grew cool again, and the shadows grew longer. Petulance and Honoriah stood on the porch and looked up at their brother.

"We're going home now," Honoriah called.

"Fine," said Frankfort.

Honoriah and Petulance shrugged their shoulders and began walking back to Merriweather Court. The bubble followed just above their heads, turning corners, occasionally swerving to avoid a street sign or a tree branch. Frankfort sat on the bottom of the bubble, arms still crossed, bouncing along, and sticking his tongue out whenever one of the twins glanced up at him.

The Freeforall children reached their street. They passed the LaCartes' house, where Della and Peony pointed at the bubble and giggled behind their hands. Honoriah opened the front door, Petulance stepped through it, and then the sisters turned back to the bubble, which was at least four feet wide.

"I guess it won't fit inside," said Honoriah, and closed the door.

Frankfort hovered over the porch.

That night the Freeforalls ate a peaceful dinner in their kitchen. The bubble now hovered outside the window. Frankfort glared in at his parents and sisters. This was uncomfortable, but no one missed his shouts of "Whatever!"

"He must be getting hungry, though," Honoriah whispered to her sister.

"I wonder if he's safe out there," Petulance replied.

After dinner the twins put in a call to Missy, who assured them that Frankfort was perfectly safe and also that he knew perfectly well how to get out of the bubble.

It wasn't until 8:30 that evening that Frankfort shouted in to his mother and asked her if she could please bring the phone outside and dial Veronica Cupcake's number. Mrs. Freeforall did so, the bubble politely floated to the ground, and when Veronica answered the phone Frankfort yelled, "Veronica, it's Frankfort Freeforall! I'm really sorry I took your hot dog. That wasn't nice of me. I'm sorry I called you a crybaby, too."

"Thank you," Veronica replied.

The bubble popped then, and Frankfort hurried inside, ate four helpings of lasagna, and went to bed.

You might think that Frankfort had seen the last of the Bubble of Apology, but over the next week, he found himself inside it seventeen more times. The nineteenth and final time occurred on the first day of school. Frankfort pouted in the bubble while he missed both gym and recess. It wasn't until two o'clock that he finally shouted, "I'm sorry I took your pen, Mrs. Berry!" and was returned to his seat in his new classroom.

At first no one realized that Frankfort's nineteenth time in the bubble was his last time. Six days went by before Mrs. Freeforall remarked to her husband, "I haven't seen that bubble in a while, have you, dear?"

Mr. Freeforall looked up from his computer. "Why no, I haven't."

"I haven't heard Frankfort say 'Whatever,' either."
Mrs. Freeforall picked up the phone. "Missy!" she
exclaimed. "I think the cure is taking effect."

What Missy wanted to say was, *Frankfort is the stub-
bornest child I've ever worked with. Who knew he'd be in
that bubble nineteen times?* What she said instead was,
"Let's start the second phase. I'll bring the pill with me
the next time I babysit for the children."

In case you've never seen one, a How-Are-You-
Doing? pill looks exactly like a gumdrop. Even so,
Frankfort was reluctant to take it. Word had gotten
around Little Spring Valley about Linden Pettigrew's
gum ball, and Frankfort didn't want to risk swallowing
something that tasted like cilantro or a dirty sponge.

"It's lemon-lime," Missy assured him, and was
greatly relieved when Frankfort finally bit into it.
It wasn't enough for Frankfort to stop thinking only
about himself. Now he needed to start thinking about
other people and how they were feeling.

The moment Frankfort swallowed the last bit of the
gumdrop, he turned to Petulance and asked enthusiastically, "How are you doing?"

Petulance, who was sitting at the kitchen table

eating a pear, was so surprised that the pear slid from her hand and splatted on the floor. "I—" she said as she fumbled for the pear, "I—why do you want to know?"

"You're my sister," Frankfort found himself replying. "How are you doing?"

"Well, I had a *pretty* good day at school, but I'm a little upset because I didn't do very well on a spelling test, and I studied really hard for it."

Frankfort felt an unfamiliar feeling spread through his body. "Are you frustrated?" he asked, frowning.

"Yes. And worried, because now Mr. Pasternak probably thinks I'm a bad speller, and I'm not."

"Hmm," said Frankfort. "I'm sorry, Petulance." He went up to his room to think things over.

All that afternoon Frankfort greeted people with a hearty, "How are you doing?"

He learned any number of interesting things. Honoriah was nervous (the good kind of nervous, she explained) because she had decided to try out for the basketball team. Missy was happy that autumn was on the way but nervous (the uncomfortable kind of nervous) because she still hadn't heard from her great-aunt.

Wag answered the question by placing his paw on Frankfort's shoulder, squinting his eyes, and concentrating. "Oh!" Frankfort exclaimed. "So that's how you feel when cats chase you. I never thought about their claws." And even though Frankfort didn't have claws, he felt bad about all the times he had chased Wag when Wag didn't want to be chased.

"How are you doing?" Frankfort yelled over the fence to Della and Peony LaCarte. They were sitting primly on their swing set.

"I'm feeling a little suspicious," Della replied, frowning at Frankfort.

"But I really want to know how you're doing."

"It's lonely over here," said Peony finally, and Frankfort decided there might be something he could do about that.

The next morning as the Freeforalls walked to school, Frankfort called out to everyone he saw, "How are you doing?!"

"Great! My grandfather is coming to visit," said Rusty Goodenough.

"Fine," replied Veronica Cupcake. "I'm going to get new sneakers this afternoon."

Frankfort checked in with Georgie Pepperpot's dog. "He's having an off day," he reported to the twins. "Something about his food."

"How are you doing?" Frankfort asked an old woman he'd never seen before.

"Just fine. Thank you for asking, young man. How charming of you."

And so it went. Frankfort asked his classmates and Mrs. Berry and the security guard and the librarian and the kindergarteners' guinea pig how they were doing. He found it especially interesting to learn that some people were unhappy or angry or frustrated or worried. He thought about that as he and his sisters walked to the upside-down house after school that day. The very first person he saw when they arrived was Melody Flowers. She was sitting by herself on the front porch, Lightfoot in her lap.

"How are you doing?" Frankfort asked her. He had the feeling that Melody might not be doing very well, so he asked the question more gently than usual.

Melody looked up at him in surprise. "Okay, I guess."

"Really?" said Frankfort. He sat beside her. Lightfoot flicked her tail in his direction.

"Well, no."

"What's the matter?"

Melody dropped her eyes and stroked Lightfoot's back. "I still feel like the new kid here," she said finally. "It's horrible being so shy."

"But everyone likes you," Frankfort told her. "You know that, don't you? My sisters always talk about how nice you are."

"They do?"

Frankfort nodded. "And so do Tulip and Veronica. Everyone, really."

Melody smiled at him. Then Frankfort glanced behind him and saw that Missy was at the door. She was smiling, too.

What Missy was thinking was that sometimes all it took was one gumdrop.

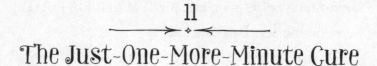

11
The Just-One-More-Minute Cure

SAMANTHA TICKLE LIVED with her parents, Trillium and Edison Tickle, in a small brown house just one block from Little Spring Valley Elementary School. Samantha had no brothers or sisters, but she had a black-and-white cat named Harley and a white-and-black cat named Jack and six goldfish that all looked exactly alike, so she hadn't bothered to name them. Samantha was a perfectly nice girl with lots of friends. She was neither too neat nor too messy, neither too polite nor too rude. She was generally helpful and thoughtful, and she took good care of the cats and the fish. Until recently, if you had asked Samantha's parents if their daughter had any bad habits, they would have frowned and looked offended and said, "Why, of course not!" They probably would have wanted to add, "Our Samantha is perfect—a little jewel of a child." But they were too modest to say such things.

All that had changed over the summer. It seemed that the more free time Samantha had in which to do whatever she pleased, the more free time she wanted. Just as the Freeforalls began to dread hearing Frankfort's "Whatever!" all day long, the Tickles began to dread Samantha's "Just one more minute!"

"Samantha, please come inside for lunch."

"Just one more minute!"

"Samantha, it's bedtime."

"Just one more minute!"

"Samantha, it's time to leave for your ballet lesson."

"Just one more minute!"

Samantha asked for "just one more minute" no matter what she was doing—playing on her computer or taking a bath or drawing pictures or lying in bed. In the evening she didn't want to go *to* bed, and in the morning she didn't want to get *out of* bed.

"What is the matter with her?" Trillium asked her

husband one evening. They had just finished eating a cold dinner. The meal had started out hot but had grown cold while they waited for Samantha, who was reading in her room, to join them. "Just one more minute!" she yelled every time they called her.

"Maybe she's becoming a teenager?" Edison suggested doubtfully as he and Trillium tidied up the kitchen.

"Is eleven considered a teenager?" replied Trillium. They didn't know.

"I'll call the LaCartes," said Edison.

This was a mistake, of course, and one that almost every parent in Little Spring Valley made from time to time. They would call the LaCartes for child-rearing advice and then hear about the perfection of Della and Peony and feel that their own children couldn't possibly measure up.

Nevertheless, Edison went ahead and made the mistake. When he got off the phone, he turned to Trillium and said, "Della and Peony never ask for one more minute. In fact, they tell their parents when it's time to leave for things like dental appointments and flu shots."

Trillium sighed. Tears came to her eyes. "Yesterday

I had to call Samantha for forty minutes before she got out of bed." She recalled how the morning had progressed.

6:30—"Samantha! Rise and shine!"

A muffled "Okay" had come from under the pillow.

6:35—"Samantha, get up, please."

"Just one more minute."

6:47—"Samantha, get up now. I'm tired of nagging you."

"Then don't nag me. I just need one more minute."

6:59—"Samantha! This is ridiculous."

"But I like my bed. And I'm still sleepy."

7:10—"Samantha. Get. Up. Now!"

"Okay!" Samantha had thrown back the covers. "You don't have to yell. I said I'd get up."

Edison Tickle put his arm around his wife. He offered her a Kleenex. "I've been hearing wonderful things about Missy Piggle-Wiggle."

"Let's call her!" Trillium said so quickly that Edison knew she'd already been thinking about calling her. "She has potions and cures and pills. All sorts of things," Trillium went on. "I wonder what she'll suggest. If it's medicine, I hope Samantha will take it without any fuss."

"I hope she'll take it without being called twelve thousand times."

Edison and Trillium sat at the kitchen table with Trillium's cell phone on speaker. When Missy answered, they explained their problem to her.

"I just can't take it anymore," Trillium said at last.

"We're losing our patience," added Edison. "Do you know that on Monday Samantha's teacher called us to say that Samantha even asks for 'just one more minute' at school?"

"Can you imagine saying 'just one more minute' to your teacher?" exclaimed Trillium. "Your *teacher*."

"So," said Edison, "do you have a potion or something for Samantha?"

"No," Missy replied.

The Tickles looked at each other in dismay.

"Nothing?" said Trillium.

"It's that bad?" said Edison.

"It's actually quite common," Missy told them.

Trillium felt a pang for all the other parents who

had been driven crazy by their children's pleas for just one more minute.

"But what do we *do*?" asked Edison.

"The next time Samantha says 'just one more minute,'" Missy began, "tell her you're not going to give her another reminder."

There was a long pause while the Tickles waited to hear the rest of the cure.

"And?" said Trillium.

"That's it," Missy replied.

"That's it?" Edison repeated.

"Well, for instance, when she asks for one more minute after you've called her for dinner, tell her that dinner will be served in five minutes and that you aren't going to give her another reminder."

"Mm-hmm, mm-hmm," said Edison.

"And then," Missy went on, "just let whatever happens happen. Go on with your dinner whether Samantha joins you or not."

Trillium winced. She didn't like the thought of her daughter missing a meal. Or arriving late to school. Or going to bed past her bedtime. Or skipping ballet class.

"There is one other thing," said Missy.

"Yes?" said the Tickles eagerly.

"You might want to pick up Penelope and have her stay at your house for a while. You're probably going to wind up leaving Samantha behind every now and then, and Penelope is an excellent babysitter."

"Penelope the parrot?" asked Edison. "How does she feel about cats? And fish?"

"She loves them," said Missy.

"All right. We'll pick her up tomorrow."

When Samantha came home from her ballet class the next afternoon, she found Penelope sitting on a perch in the Tickles' living room. She stroked her tail feathers. "What's Penelope doing here?" she asked her father.

"Just visiting."

"Cool," said Samantha.

Penelope burst into raucous squawks.

"She sounds like she's laughing," Samantha remarked.

That evening Trillium and Edison prepared a wonderful meal. They were gourmet cooks, and Samantha had grown up eating béarnaise sauce and quail eggs and Stilton cheese and lime curd and other things that would make most children hold their noses and squinch up their eyes. Tonight they had prepared lemongrass chicken and crab bisque.

"Samantha!" Trillium called when the meal was almost ready. "Dinnertime!"

"Just one more minute!" shouted Samantha, who was in her bedroom playing on the computer.

"All right, but dinner is going to be on the table in five minutes, and I'm not going to give you another reminder."

Samantha's voice floated down the stairs again, this time sounding somewhat vague. "Kay-ay."

Edison and Trillium carried the dishes into the dining room. Penelope flew in behind them and perched on the back of Samantha's chair. Edison ladled the bisque into bowls, and Trillium served the chicken.

Trillium looked at her watch. "It's been five minutes," she said.

"Plenty of time!" said Penelope, ruffling her feathers. "Plenty!"

Edison shrugged his shoulders. He picked up his fork and began eating. Eventually, Trillium did the same.

They finished the meal. Twenty minutes had passed since they'd called Samantha.

They were reading in the living room when Samantha ambled downstairs. "Hey," she said. "What's going on? I thought it was dinnertime."

"It was," her father replied. "So we ate."

"Already? What about my dinner?"

"It's on the table."

Samantha peeked into the dining room. Penelope was still perched on the back of her chair. "Do you like cold food?" she squawked. "Do you like cold food?"

Samantha examined her meal. "Everything *is* cold!" she exclaimed. "The sauce is all, like, congealed. And there's scum on top of the soup."

"I don't think it will hurt you," said her mother.

Samantha slid into her place, and Penelope fluttered across the table to Trillium's chair. Samantha skimmed the scum off the bisque and set it aside. She tasted the soup. She made a face. "I don't like cold bisque!" she called to her parents.

Trillium continued reading. "Heat it up," she replied.

Samantha sighed. "Maybe I'll just make a sandwich."

"Okay," said Edison, and added, "don't forget to clear your place and load the dishwasher."

Samantha banged her way into the kitchen, mumbling things about parents and schedules and people who don't care what their children eat.

"What's that? What's that?" cried Penelope. "Speak up, girl!"

Samantha ate a peanut-butter sandwich that stuck to the roof of her mouth and then stalked through the living room, saying, "I really enjoyed all the extra computer time. Thank you."

Up in her room she tackled her homework and then went back to the computer. At nine thirty Trillium called to her, "Samantha! Time to get ready for bed. Tomorrow is the field trip to the wildlife preserve, and you don't want to be tired for it."

"Just one more minute!" called Samantha.

Trillium winced. She had hoped that maybe her daughter would already be cured. However, she said bravely, "Okay, but I'm not giving you another warning."

Samantha didn't answer.

At ten o'clock the Tickles put away their books and

turned on the news. Edison looked at Penelope, who was dozing on her perch. "Do you sleep there?" he asked.

Penelope fluttered lazily upstairs. "I'll sleep in Samantha's room," she replied.

Trillium and Edison watched the news. Then they locked the doors and turned off the lights. They tiptoed upstairs—and were dismayed to see that although Samantha's door was closed, her light was shining beneath it. They could hear the computer keys clicking away.

"We must be strong," said Edison, and he and Trillium went to bed.

At eleven thirty Samantha's eyes began to close, but since no one had said anything else to her about bedtime, she played three more games. At last she fell into bed. "Wow," she said. "It's after midnight."

"Quiet, girl," Penelope replied. "I'm trying to sleep."

The next morning Trillium knocked on Samantha's door. "Time to get up. Field trip day!" When she heard no answer, she opened the door and said more loudly, "Time to get up!"

"Just one more minute," murmured Samantha, who felt as if she had been asleep for barely an hour.

"Okay, but I'm not going to give you another reminder."

"Mmphh."

The Tickles left for work. The next time Samantha opened her eyes, it was nearly eleven. She found Penelope standing on her pillow, staring at her.

"It's about time," Penelope squawked.

Samantha shrieked. Then she cried, "You scared me!" and after that she cried, "I missed the field trip! The buses left at eight thirty."

"Hmm. What a pickle," said Penelope.

"Why didn't Mom wake me up?"

"She did. Come on. Breakfast time. I'm starving."

Samantha sat glumly in the kitchen. "There's no point in going to school now," she told Penelope. "Everyone's at the preserve." Then she brightened. "My art supplies!" she exclaimed. "I can spend the day making stuff."

And she did. She was perfectly happy until the doorbell rang at three thirty, and who did she find standing

on the porch but Melody, Tulip, Honoriah, and Petulance. They all began talking at once.

"What happened? Were you sick?"

"We saw owls and foxes and a baby raccoon!"

"And wild turkeys and three different kinds of snakes."

"We ate lunch at a snack bar and got cotton candy."

"We bought rubber snakes in the gift shop."

"Any parrots?" screeched Penelope. "Did you see any parrots?"

Samantha tried to convince herself that a day spent making a cardboard town was just as good as a trip to see wild animals and buy cotton candy.

The week wore on. Samantha missed another day of school by sleeping until lunchtime after watching hours of late-night television.

"Wow. It's almost one o'clock," said Samantha when she finally woke up, bright sunshine pouring through the blinds.

"What a shock," said Penelope.

Trillium and Edison were at work, of course, so Samantha and Penelope spent the afternoon together.

The doorbell rang at three thirty, and Samantha was astonished to find her teacher on the stoop. Mrs. Gnash handed her a folder. "Here's today's work," she said. "Everything we did in class, plus your homework. Also, you still need to hand in the essay that was assigned after the field trip."

"Oh!" said Samantha. She felt a little overwhelmed.

On Thursday Samantha made it to school and was only fifteen minutes late. Mrs. Gnash said to her, "You're late, Samantha."

"My mom only told me to get up once."

In the front of the room, Della LaCarte raised her hand. "My parents never have to tell me anything twice."

"Thank you, Della," said Mrs. Gnash.

Samantha flumped into her seat and stuck her tongue out at the back of Della's head.

That night when Trillium Tickle knocked on Samantha's door and said, "Time to start your homework," Samantha replied, "Okay!"

Trillium ran downstairs to report this happy turn of events to Edison.

Upstairs, Samantha looked around for her work folders. It had become difficult to find anything. All week long Edison and Trillium had said to her, "Time to clean up your room," and Samantha had replied, "Just one more minute," and then gone back to her art projects or her computer. Now her floor was a sea of papers and markers and beads and books and blankets and shoes. Her bed wasn't any better, and the pile of dirty clothes on her desk chair was so tall that earlier in the day, Harley had tried to jump on it, and the clothes had toppled over and buried him. Samantha had unburied him and thrown the clothes back on the chair. Now she looked around in vain for her work folders.

"I can't find them!" she complained to Penelope. "I can't find anything."

"It's quite a pigsty."

The weekend rolled around, and Samantha was relieved. She spent all of Saturday trying to catch up on her missed homework assignments. At six o'clock she ambled into the kitchen. "What's for dinner?" she asked her parents.

"We're going to eat out," Edison replied.

"Why?"

"It's impossible to cook."

Samantha took a look around the kitchen. It was her job to load the dishwasher, and she hadn't done it once all week. Every single dish, glass, bowl, and pan was piled in the sink and spilling out over the counters. They were all dirty, and not a single clean dish, glass, bowl, or pan was left in the cupboards. There was nothing to cook with and nothing to eat on.

"Can I come with you?" asked Samantha in a small voice.

"Sure, but we're leaving in two minutes."

Samantha ran to her room. "I just need to change my clothes," she called over her shoulder.

She looked at the pile of dirty things on the chair. There wasn't much left in her closet. She pulled a shirt out from the pile and sniffed it. "Ew."

"EW!" squawked Penelope. Then she added, "One more minute. Just one more minute until they leave."

Samantha sniffed at a few other shirts, found nothing clean, shrugged, and began to pick her way through the mess on the floor. She tripped over a tiara, landed on the Monopoly board, and sat for a moment rubbing her elbow. By the time she reached the front door, the Tickles' car was cruising down the street.

This is how Samantha suddenly knew she was growing up: She didn't cry. She didn't accuse her parents of torturing her or abandoning her. She simply said, "All right. I'll make my own dinner." She checked the contents of the refrigerator. "Pasta with vegetables, I think."

She pulled a large pot out from the mountain in the sink, and the entire mountain went crashing and clanging to the floor. Pots rolled under the table. Pans skidded across the linoleum. One plate broke.

"Huh. Look at that," said Penelope.

Samantha, still feeling grown-up, walked calmly to the cabinet where the cleaning supplies were stored and began to put the kitchen back in order. She swept and scrubbed and washed and dried.

"You go, girl," said Penelope.

Samantha smiled at her.

When Edison and Trillium returned two hours

later, they found a clean house, the dishwasher humming, and Samantha finishing up her homework while Penelope dozed on her perch.

Trillium reached for her phone and called Missy.

"Thank you," she said.

12

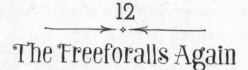

The Freeforalls Again

IT WAS A blustery October afternoon. Missy Piggle-Wiggle sat on the porch of the upside-down house, having coffee with Lester. She watched yellow maple leaves whoosh along the path to the front door. It was time for leaf raking and pumpkin carving.

Across Little Spring Valley, the Freeforalls sat in a row on their front stoop, Honoriah and Petulance on either end, Frankfort between them. The air smelled of wood smoke and damp earth. The children sat silently, chins in hands.

At the upside-down house Missy said to Lester, "If only grown-ups were as easy to cure as children."

On Merriweather Court, Petulance lifted her head and said, "I wish it were tomorrow instead of today."

"Why?" asked Frankfort.

"Because tomorrow is Thursday, and Missy comes on Thursdays."

"Let's go to Missy's, then," said Honoriah, and of course all three children jumped to their feet.

Frankfort and his sisters had never had a friend like Missy. They no longer hooted at her if she said *rear*. They wouldn't *think* of groaning when she appeared at their door. And they didn't mind in the least that she had shrunk Petulance's possessions or given Honoriah a cure for know-it-alls or placed Frankfort in a slimy, unbreakable bubble. Missy was the best friend they had ever had. Who else carried around a magic bag full of art supplies and had a pig who drank coffee and a goose named Evelyn and a house with its feet in the air? Who else told them stories and taught them to cook and kept them so busy that they didn't need to fight anymore?

Nobody.

The Freeforalls called good-bye to their mother, hopped on their bicycles, and rode across town.

"Remember our sleepover at Missy's?" said Frankfort as they pedaled along.

"Which one?" asked Honoriah.

"The one when we dressed up like old-timey people and had high tea for dinner."

"How about the time Wag slept with me and Lightfoot slept with Petulance and Lester slept by your bed and got you a drink of water in the middle of the night?"

"My favorite sleepover," said Petulance, "was when we had the pirate dance in the basement—"

"You mean the attic," said Frankfort.

"The basement-attic, and Missy showed us real gold doubloons."

The Freeforalls rode on.

At the upside-down house, Missy got to her feet. "Company is on the way," she said to Lester. "I can feel it in my bones."

Lester nodded thoughtfully.

Missy stretched, collected the coffee cups, carried them into the kitchen, and returned to the porch. She was wearing a thick sweater. Even so, she rubbed her hands together. "Chilly," she said. "Pretty soon it will be time to put away my straw hat and get out the wool one." She was quiet for a moment, then sighed and said, "Now about curing grown-ups. How on earth am I going to fix Mr. and Mrs. Freeforall?"

Lester shrugged his hairy shoulders.

"Well, I'm not going to worry about it," said Missy after another moment. "Something will come to me." She stepped to the edge of the porch. "They're almost here," she told Lester.

At that moment, three bicycles turned the corner and flew along the road to the upside-down house. The twins and Frankfort tossed their bikes on the lawn and unstrapped their helmets. They ran to Missy and hugged her. Then they hugged Lester, who gave them a polite piggy smile.

"Missy, we have an idea!" exclaimed Honoriah.

"We just got it now," said Petulance.

"While we were riding over here," added Frankfort.

"Goodness," said Missy. "You'd better tell me what it is before you explode."

"Could we turn your house into a haunted mansion for our parents?" Petulance blurted out.

"I wanted to say that!" cried Frankfort.

"It's a wonderful idea," Missy said, putting her

arm across Frankfort's shoulders, "and I know you all thought it up together. How clever of you." She tapped her finger on her forehead and thought, *This might be just what is needed.*

"We could show Mom and Dad our pumpkins," said Frankfort.

"And our Halloween costumes," said Honoriah.

Petulance opened the front door. "Let's go inside and work on our costumes now."

The Freeforall children had never made their costumes before. In past years they had ridden glumly to Juniper Street with their mother or father, rushed into Aunt Martha's General Store, picked through the boxes of premade costumes and plastic masks, and fought over who got what.

This year would be different.

There was no place like the upside-down house for making Halloween costumes. The Freeforalls discovered that everywhere they looked, they found another carton labeled WIGS or NOSES or EYE PATCHES. Their favorite box was labeled FANGS AND TEETH. They had all hunted through the house many times on rainy days during the summer and were certain they hadn't seen the boxes before.

"Hey!" exclaimed Petulance on that blustery Wednesday. "Here's a box called WINGS AND WANDS."

"Ooh, and here's a tube of fake blood," said Honoriah, squirting some across her face. "How do I look?"

"I thought you were going to be a princess," said Frankfort.

"Maybe I'll be a princess who's just been in a car accident."

"That's the wonderful thing about Halloween," said Missy. "You can be whatever you want to be."

Lester stepped into the dining room, where the Freeforalls were sitting around the table, hunched over their costumes. He carried a tray with glasses of milk and a plate of doughnuts.

"Why, thank you, Lester," said Missy. "How thoughtful of you."

"Yes, thank you," echoed the twins.

"We need a break," added Frankfort.

"Now tell me about the haunted mansion," said Missy as Lester joined them at the table.

"It will be a surprise for Mom and Dad," said Frank-fort.

"We'll decorate it with witches and ghosts and monsters," said Petulance.

"And our pumpkins," said Honoriah. "All lit up."

"We'll have it at the end of the day when it's dark and spooky out."

"We'll hang threads from the ceiling so Mom and Dad will feel like they're walking through cobwebs."

"We'll make a tape of scary sounds. Screams and bangs and laughter. *Mwa-ha-ha-ha*."

"We'll wear our costumes," said Petulance.

"Mom and Dad will be amazed," said Frankfort. He crawled into Missy's lap. "Don't you think they'll be amazed?"

"Well, they certainly ought to be," replied Missy, and tugged her hat into place. "Maybe we'll ask Harold to help us. He's decorating his store for Halloween, and he always has creative ideas."

"Will you call Mom today?" asked Honoriah.

As usual, Mrs. Hudson Freeforall was sitting in front of the computer in her home office. She had not noticed the blustery day or the yellow tumbling leaves or the smell of wood smoke. Her back was facing the window; otherwise she might have noticed the bare branch scraping the pane and perhaps thought of Halloweens from her childhood. What she did notice was the quiet. It had been a long time since the twins and Frankfort had slid screaming down the banister or thrown a baseball at the china cabinet or turned the bathtub into a swimming pool. The children had ridden their bikes to Missy's house, but lately, even when they were at home, they did their chores or their homework, and they rarely fought or threw things over the fence into the LaCartes' yard. They were turning into nice, predictable, well-mannered children.

Mrs. Freeforall thought about her changed children for four grateful seconds and then went back to work. The phone rang. "Hello?" she said. "Missy, is that you? Is everything all right?"

"Everything is fine."

At the upside-down house, Missy sat in an armchair beside a window, her sweater draped across her shoulders. From the dining room drifted the voices of

Honoriah, Petulance, and Frankfort as they worked on their costumes.

"Well, then?" said Mrs. Freeforall, and her eyes focused on the computer screen again.

"The children want to issue an invitation to you and Mr. Freeforall. They're planning a Halloween surprise for you. They've been working on their costumes and carving pumpkins, and they want to show everything off to you here at the upside-down house."

"Mmm-hmm."

Missy heard the clacking of computer keys. "Will you be able to come?" she asked, somewhat more loudly than was necessary.

"To what?" said Mrs. Freeforall. "I mean, of course. Of course we'll come. When is . . . it?"

"Next Friday at four o'clock. The day before Halloween."

"Mmm-hmm."

"Mrs. Freeforall?"

"Hudson will have to leave work early."

"I know, but this will mean a lot to the children."

"All right. We'll be there."

The upside-down house had never seen so much

activity. All week the children of Little Spring Valley worked to make the best haunted mansion they could imagine. Mr. and Mrs. Freeforall were invited for Friday afternoon. Everyone else was invited for Saturday.

"A haunted house on Halloween!" exclaimed Melody in a voice so loud she surprised even herself.

"An upside-down haunted house," said Veronica. "I'll bet it's the only one in town."

"You should charge money," Rusty said to Missy.

"You won't serve gum, will you?" asked Linden.

Frankfort, Petulance, and Honoriah put the finishing touches on their costumes. "Do you think Mom and Dad will know I'm a princess who's been in a car accident?" asked Honoriah.

"I'm sure they will," Missy replied.

On Friday the Freeforall children rode their bicycles directly to Missy's after school. "Three o'clock," Petulance declared when they arrived. "Only one hour until Mom and Dad get here."

Penelope was so excited about all the activity that she announced the Freeforalls before they even rang the bell. "Honoriah, Petulance, and Frankfort are here for the haunted mansion!" she cried.

Missy answered the door dressed as a witch. Behind her was Lester wearing a top hat and a bow tie, behind him was Wag in a bunny suit, and behind *him* sat Lightfoot, halfway up the stairs.

"What happened to Lightfoot's costume?" asked Frankfort.

"She refused to let me put it on her."

"Just like a cat!" squawked Penelope, who was perched on a chandelier and not wearing a costume, either.

"Come on. Time for the finishing touches," said Petulance. "Let's get to work."

At four o'clock Missy the witch was sitting on the couch in the parlor with a princess who'd been in a car accident, the Baby New Year, and a can of soup. On a table in front of them were a dish of candy corn, a plate of pumpkin cookies, and a bowl of apples. The lights had been turned down, cobwebs swung from the ceilings, and monsters were propped up in dark corners. Through the open window, Missy could hear an owl hoot.

"Everything is set for our victims," whispered Frankfort. *"Mwa-ha-ha-ha!"*

"Do you hear a car? I think I hear a car," said Petulance. She rushed to the window. But the car drove by the upside-down house and kept on going.

Four fifteen came and went.

Four thirty came and went.

"They're half an hour late," said Petulance.

"They forgot," said Honoriah.

"I knew they'd forget," said Frankfort.

Nobody spoke for a few minutes, and then Honoriah said in a small voice, "I don't think they care about us."

"We aren't as important as their work," added Petulance.

"I wish they didn't *have* their jobs!" said Frankfort.

Missy looked at them thoughtfully. "Your parents work hard to support you," she said finally. "They want to make a good life for you."

Frankfort reached for Wag and pulled him onto his lap. Wag's feet spilled over onto the couch, but he rested his head on Frankfort's arm and turned mournful eyes on him.

The twins looked around at the haunted mansion. They looked at their costumes and at their pumpkins, glowing in the front windows.

"They forgot about us," said Frankfort again.

Honoriah let out a sigh. "Missy, could we come here and live with you?"

"Oh yes, *could* we?" asked Petulance.

"Please could we?" said Frankfort.

"You have plenty of extra rooms," Honoriah pointed out.

"*You* would never forget about us," said Frankfort.

"We would do anything you say," added Petulance. "Anything at all. Give us a chore, and we would do it. Without complaining."

Missy heard a small noise from the front porch and glanced at the open window. She turned back to the Freeforalls. "What about your parents?" she asked. "Don't you think they would miss you?"

Frankfort shook his head. "Not really."

"If they missed us, they would have been here half an hour ago," said Honoriah.

"If they didn't have us, they could just work, work, work all the time," said Frankfort. "Then they'd be happy."

Petulance cocked her head. "Did you hear something?" she whispered suddenly. "I heard a noise."

"You have Halloween fever," her sister replied.

"No, I did hear something." Petulance ran to the window. Two shadowy figures stood in the dark. "Aughh!" she screamed before she realized that the figures were her own parents. "Mom and Dad!" she exclaimed.

Frankfort jumped to his feet and ran to open the front door. "You're here! You remembered!" he said.

"Penelope didn't announce you," said Honoriah, frowning.

"Come in and sit down," said Missy quietly.

"But I want to show them the haunted mansion," said Frankfort.

"In a minute, buddy," said Mr. Freeforall. "First, can we talk about what you said just now?"

Honoriah had crossed her arms. "You heard?" she asked her parents.

"Yes," said Mrs. Freeforall.

"Why were you late?" demanded Petulance.

"*Did* you forget?" asked Frankfort.

Mrs. Freeforall sat on a chair by the fireplace. Her husband sat next to her. The chairs had been coated with baby powder so that they poofed dustily whenever the Freeforalls moved. Cobwebs tickled their hair and faces.

Before anyone could say anything else, Lester got to his feet and left the room.

"Was that a pig?" asked Mr. Freeforall.

"Yes. He's probably fixing you something to drink," said Missy.

Mrs. Freeforall looked at her children. Her eyes grew bright, and she wiped them with a tissue. "Did you mean what you were saying?"

"Yes," replied Petulance, Frankfort, and Honoriah.

"You would really rather live here," said their father, looking around at the chandelier that grew out of the floor and Penelope, who was perched on Frankfort's head, and the dust rising from the chairs, "than at home with your mother and me?"

There was a long silence, and finally Honoriah said in a small voice, "Missy's always at home—"

"But we *have* to work," their mother interrupted. "We have to earn money to buy food and clothes and to pay for the house."

"But do you have to work at night and on the

weekends?" asked Petulance. "You're *always* working. Or going on business trips."

"I think," said Missy, "that your children feel forgotten. They feel hurt."

Mrs. Freeforall put her hand to her mouth. "We didn't mean to hurt you!"

"And we do think about you," said their father, who had reached for his handkerchief. "We only want what's best for you."

"*You're* best for us," said Honoriah.

"Then we'll make some changes," said Mrs. Freeforall. "We promise."

"We'll do whatever it takes," agreed their father.

"Even turn off your phones at dinnertime?" asked Honoriah.

"Definitely," said Mrs. Freeforall.

The twins and Frankfort suddenly stood up and flew across the room to their parents. Missy had never seen so much hugging and apologizing and crying in her life.

"Oh my," said Mrs. Freeforall after a while. "Where's that pig? I could use a glass of water."

~~~~~

Eventually everyone settled down, and Mr. and Mrs. Freeforall were given the tour of the haunted house. They jumped and screamed at all the right times, and they admired the costumes and the pumpkins and expressed amazement at their children's hard work. When at last the Freeforall family left for their home, Missy plopped down on the couch and rested her feet on a cushion.

"What an evening," she said to Lester, who was sitting across the room. Then she added, "It looks like I'm out of a job. The Freeforalls won't need a sitter anymore."

Lester nodded and smiled.

"And, House," Missy went on, talking to the air, "thank you for letting the children coat you with powder and turn you into a haunted mansion."

The front door creaked open. Missy guessed that meant *You're welcome*.

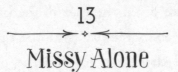

13

Missy Alone

IT WAS A quiet Saturday in Little Spring Valley. Halloween had come and gone, and Thanksgiving was less than two weeks away. The warm weather was over, and the trees were bare, the last of their red and gold leaves lying wetly in gutters. The tourists and weekend visitors had stopped making trips to Juniper Street for ice-cream cones and handmade candles, or to ooh and aah over the windows at Aunt Martha's General Store. On Spell Street, the Art of Magic had closed its doors until spring.

At the upside-down house, Missy built a fire in the

fireplace most evenings. She admired the thick winter coats the animals had grown.

"Where are the children today?" she wondered now. She looked at Lester, who shrugged his shoulders. "It's a lovely day, but it's so quiet." She thought about her great-aunt, who would have said, "Such a time and no one to it."

"Should I be worried?" Missy asked Lester. She was sitting in the parlor, her feet propped up on the chandelier. Wag was curled beside her, and Lightfoot was curled in her lap, purring. "Month after month without a word from my great-aunt, and today not a soul has come to the door."

"You have *us!*" screeched Penelope from her perch.

"So I do," said Missy. Still, something was missing. "What could it be?" she asked.

Lester looked at her and shook his head. Missy could cure any child in town, but when it came to her own problems, she was . . .

"Clueless!" cried Penelope, bouncing up and down. "Clueless!"

Missy stood, walked through the kitchen, and let

herself out the back door. "Hello, Warren. Hello, Evelyn. Hello, Martha," she said, stepping around the geese and the duck as she made her way to the barn. "Hello, Trotsky. Hello, Heather," she said to the horse and the cow in their stalls. She tipped her head back and called hello to Pulitzer in the rafters.

"Whoo," murmured the owl, since Missy was interrupting his sleep.

Missy looked around at the neat barn and the tidy yard. She sighed. "Nothing to do here." She walked back to the house. In the parlor she said, "You know, Lester, I think maybe I'm just a bit lonely. I think maybe I need to see a friend."

Lester nodded wisely, and Penelope shouted, "At last! At last!" Then she swooped across the room, picked up Missy's wool hat in her claws, and deposited it on Missy's head. "Go!"

The house opened the front door, Lester handed Missy her pocketbook, and before she knew it, she was hurrying along the path to the sidewalk.

"Blue sky," Missy murmured to herself. "Cool air. No wind. A perfect autumn day."

Missy walked toward Juniper Street and began to

hum. She turned the corner. Why, she would just take herself down the block to A to Z Books and have a chat with Harold. That ought to cheer her up. Missy approached the store and had put out her hand to open the door, expecting to hear the sneeze, when the door suddenly opened from the other side and Harold stepped out.

"Missy!" he exclaimed.

"Harold! You startled me."

"I'm sorry," said Harold. He stuffed his hands in his pockets.

"Where are you off to?" asked Missy. "Closing up early?"

Harold shook his head. "Business is slow, but I left Benny in charge in case someone needs a book." He tilted his head toward the sun. "I decided it's too nice to stay inside, so I'm giving myself the afternoon off. I'm going to take a walk around town. Where are *you* off to?"

Missy shrugged. "I'm not sure."

Harold held his hand out to her. "Care to join me? I did promise to take you on a tour of the town."

"I would love to," Missy replied. She took Harold's

hand, and off they went down Juniper Street, Missy in her wild, wrinkled coat and her wool hat, a pair of green high-heeled boots on her feet, and Harold in his red top hat and tuxedo and his purple shoes. He carried the cane in his free hand, and it went *tip-tip-tip-tip* along the sidewalk.

For a while, Harold and Missy ambled through town, turning a corner here, a corner there, Harold telling her interesting bits about Little Spring Valley. They passed Rusty Goodenough's house, where they saw him playing catch in his yard with Tulip and not spying on anyone. They passed Heavenly Earwig's house, where they saw her run through her front door and heard her mother call from inside, "Oh good. You're right on time!" They passed Linden Pettigrew's house, where they saw him sitting on his front stoop eating an apple.

"So many happy children," said Harold to Missy, and he squeezed her hand.

"Hmm," said Missy, who was thinking of I Never-Said-itis and Just-One-More-Minuters and alarms and enormous gum balls.

"There's something wonderful about Little Spring Valley," Harold went on.

Missy cocked her head at him. "Is there?"

"Yes. But it's hard to describe."

"I have a feeling in my bones," said Missy as she steered Harold toward a large park at the edge of town. "I feel as though something magical could happen at any moment."

Harold laughed. "I know what you mean."

Missy paused then, just for a fraction of a second. Just long enough for Harold to think maybe she had lost her footing or seen something out of the corner of her eye. And then they were walking along again, smiling, hand in hand, Harold's cane going *tip-tip-tip-tip.*

Ahead of them was a line of trees, and beyond the trees was Edgewood Park. Missy and Harold could hear the squeaking of swings and the shrieks of children hanging from monkey bars. They could smell hot dogs roasting and marshmallows toasting.

Harold came to a sudden stop. "Well, I never," he said softly. "Look at that. A hot-air balloon!"

The balloon, taller than a house, was striped red and white, like a peppermint stick, and a small gold pennant flew from the top. Daisies studded the rim of the gondola, looped together with crimson ribbon.

A man with a large round Santa Claus–like belly approached Harold and Missy.

"Where did he come from?" asked Harold. "I didn't see him before. Just the balloon. And then all of a sudden, there he was."

The man was wearing a lavender brocade vest with daisies for buttons and little shoes with toes that curled upward and ended in bells.

"He looks like a jester," Harold whispered to Missy. "Or an elf."

Missy personally felt that someone wearing a red top hat and carrying a cane for no reason shouldn't comment on what anyone else was wearing, but she simply smiled.

"Balloon rides!" called the man. "The adventure of a lifetime!"

"Did you hear anything about balloon rides today?" Harold asked Missy. "You'd think it would have been in the paper."

Missy smiled again and shrugged her shoulders. She felt like Lester.

"Well, let's go!" cried Harold. "We can't miss out on the adventure of a lifetime."

He pulled Missy toward the man, who said, "Abercrombie Terwilliger, at your service."

"How much is a ride?" asked Harold. He began fumbling in his pocket.

"For you and Missy Piggle-Wiggle—free," said Abercrombie.

Harold turned to Missy. "You know him?"

"We're two peas in a pod" was Missy's reply. "Now, let's not look a gift horse in the mouth. Come along. Abercrombie is offering us a ride for free."

Abercrombie extended his hand to Missy and helped her into the basket. Harold followed her, and before he knew it, they were floating gently above Little Spring Valley, the park growing smaller and smaller beneath them.

"Just pretend I'm not here," said Abercrombie. He handed Missy and Harold a picnic basket, and then he appeared to fall asleep.

Harold peeked into the basket. "Hot chocolate and

cake and biscuits and roast chicken," he said. "This is quite a picnic." He glanced at the sleeping Abercrombie. "I hope he knows what he's doing."

"I'm certain he does," replied Missy. She peered over the rim of the gondola. "Look, there's Juniper Street and A to Z Books."

"There are the school and the library."

"There's the Freeforalls' house."

"There's your house, Missy!"

Missy looked where Harold was pointing. She could make out the upside-down house, squatting before the pasture and the barnyard. "Oh dear," said Missy. "Trotsky has let himself out of his stall again."

"Pulitzer will keep him in line," said Harold. "Don't you worry."

"Pulitzer is asleep."

"So is Abercrombie," Harold pointed out, glancing at the fat little man, who was dozing with his chin resting on his chest.

Missy looped her arm through Harold's. "This is lovely, the best kind of tour. I always like seeing things from above. There's nothing like viewing your life from a different perspective."

The balloon bobbed along. Missy and Harold sat on benches in the gondola and ate their unexpected picnic.

"Who knew," said Harold, "that one day I'd be sitting in a balloon with you high above town drinking hot chocolate?"

"There's magic everywhere you look," Missy replied.

Just as they were swallowing the last of the hot chocolate, Abercrombie snorted himself awake and began to release air from the balloon. The sun was low in the sky and the chilly air felt even chillier.

"Time to land," said Abercrombie, and before they knew it the balloon was bumping lightly down into Edgewood Park.

"It looks like everyone has gone home," said Harold, and Missy thought he sounded sad.

"Day is done," Missy replied practically.

Abercrombie alighted from the gondola and helped Missy and Harold to the ground.

"Thank you, Abercrombie!" called Missy as she and Harold walked through the fallen leaves.

"I feel I should pay him something," said Harold. "Should I pay him?" He turned around and saw nothing but trees and slides and swings and the ball field. "He's gone! Abercrombie is gone and so is the balloon. How did that happen?"

Missy once again looped her arm through Harold's. She patted his hand. "That was an afternoon to remember."

"Yes," said Harold, and he scratched his head.

Missy and Harold walked back to Juniper Street. When they reached A to Z Books, Harold went inside to help Benny close the shop. "See you tomorrow?" he asked Missy. "I could drop by."

"See you tomorrow," she replied.

Missy walked back to the upside-down house. Every few steps she skipped a little. She passed Melody's and saw her climbing into the car with her father. "I'm going to a sleepover at Tulip's!" called Melody.

Missy skipped along. She reached the upside-down house and hurried down the walk. As she stepped onto the porch, the house gallantly opened the front door for her.

"Thank you," said Missy.

Lester hurried to Missy's side and pointed at something on the table in the front hallway.

"Ah, the mail," said Missy. She picked up a handful of envelopes. The address on the very first one was in Mrs. Piggle-Wiggle's loopy handwriting.

"Auntie!" exclaimed Missy, and she opened the envelope.

Dear Missy,

I'm sorry you haven't heard from me in such a long while. I didn't expect to be out of touch for this long. Pirates are so unpredictable. I wish I could tell you where I am, but that isn't possible. I believe I am close to finding Mr. Piggle-Wiggle, and I don't want to put him in danger.

I hope all is well at the upside-down house. I miss Wag and Lightfoot and Lester and the others, but I know you've caring for them as well as I would. Can you stay in Little Spring Valley a bit longer? If you're running low on money, look for the silver key in the attic.

It means a great deal to me that I can trust you.

In haste,
Auntie

Interview with
ANN M. MARTIN and
ANNIE PARNELL
about
Missy Piggle-Wiggle

interviewed by STACY CONRADT
of Mental Floss

How did the idea to reboot Mrs. Piggle-Wiggle come about?

Ann M. Martin: I was an avid fan. I had the first four Mrs. Piggle-Wiggle books, which I can envision on the shelf in my bedroom. The stories made me laugh out loud. My favorite was *The Radish Cure*, in which a little girl who doesn't like taking baths is allowed *not* to bathe for so long that her body becomes encased with soil, at which point her parents are instructed to plant radish seeds in the dirt one night. Several days later she finds herself covered with green sprouts, and begs for a bath. Problem solved. Brilliant. So when my editors told me that Annie Parnell was interested in bringing back the world of Mrs. Piggle-Wiggle and asked if I'd be interested in writing the books, of course I said yes.

Annie Parnell: The reboot of the series was a long time coming. Back, before I had kids, when I worked in the television industry, I spent a fair amount of my free time trying to crack a way into bringing Mrs. Piggle-Wiggle to the screen. It might seem easy, but when you really dig in and look at the books, Mrs. Piggle-Wiggle simply isn't in them that much. Which begs the question: How do you make a TV series or movie when the title character just isn't there? It wasn't until after I had kids of my own that I saw Betty's stories from an entirely new perspective. It was then that I realized if I were to ever reimagine this world on the page or the screen, I wanted to spend a lot more time in the wonderful, sometimes magical, upside-down world of the Piggle-Wiggles.

However, I didn't want to reinvent Mrs. Piggle-Wiggle. She really is perfect the way she is, so Missy seemed like a natural way back into these stories. And, of course, none of this would have ever happened if it wasn't for my brilliant manager, Rachel Miller (who also happens to be a Piggle-Wiggle fanatic). She really gave me that first big push away from the screen and back to the page.

You've succeeded in maintaining the tone and overall Piggle-Wiggle magic while still updating the series for today's kids. Were you concerned about walking that line?

AM: I was more concerned about doing justice to the world that Betty MacDonald had created. Hers are big shoes to fill. But I had so much fun with that world and its magic that my stage fright faded as I worked on the first book. Annie Parnell had lots of ideas about updating the series and about the introduction of Missy Piggle-Wiggle, and she, [Feiwel & Friends publisher] Jean Feiwel, [Feiwel & Friends editor-in-chief] Liz Szabla, and I met and talked often about the direction the new series should take, so I felt well supported when I began writing.

How closely did you two work together?

AM: It was Annie's idea to introduce Missy, Mrs. Piggle-Wiggle's great-niece, a younger and more contemporary character. Annie, Jean, Liz, and I met early on to talk about Missy and how she would fit into the world of Mrs. Piggle-Wiggle. The four of us spoke several more times by phone, and Annie read and commented on the outline for the book as well as each stage of the manuscript. She had fun ideas for cures and, as a mom, she also had valuable insight into the problems kids encounter today.

AP: Working with Ann was great. Creating the world and setting up the rules was a wholly collaborative process, with lots of back and forth, pitching ideas for cures and characters and storylines. But when it comes down to it, Ann did the heavy lifting here. She's the one who sat down in front of the blank page day after day and wrote a book, and somehow managed to step into

Betty's shoes and run in them. She really did a spectacular job. This is not to say that I didn't have some very strong opinions about how some of the stories played out, I absolutely did, but fortunately everyone involved in the project wanted the same thing: a book that is fun and funny that holds true to the world that Betty created without feeling too old-fashioned, and I feel really confident that we did that.

Ann, you've talked before about how your characters are often inspired by people you know. Kristy and Mary Anne from The Baby-Sitters Club, for example, included characteristics from you and your best friend. Is Missy inspired by anyone?

AM: Being able to build on the world created by Betty MacDonald is great fun. Missy wasn't inspired by anyone in particular, but the Piggle-Wiggle world is in my mind when I write. In fact, I keep copies of the books on my desk for inspiration.

Did Betty MacDonald leave anything for you to work with—storylines or characters cut from previous books?

AM: No, I didn't have any unpublished work, but I did have that fabulous world—the upside-down house, Lester the polite pig, Penelope the parrot, and the other animals. And of course Mrs. Piggle-Wiggle's particular way of dealing with children, which manages to be both practical and magical, not to mention hilarious.

AP: As far as I know, Betty only left one unpublished cure, which my grandmother, Anne Canham, incorporated into her book, *Happy Birthday, Mrs. Piggle-Wiggle*. But I think Betty's published material, and a lifetime of my family making up their own little Piggle-Wiggle-esque cures and stories, was more than enough to send us on the right track.

With your grandmother also working on the Piggle-Wiggle series, was there a "passing of the torch," so to speak?

AP: My grandmother was thrilled when I proposed writing a new series of books and has been my number one cheerleader this entire time. I honestly couldn't have done it without her support and steadfast belief in me.

Inventing the various Piggle-Wiggle cures and potions seems like it would be a blast. If you could invent your own Piggle-Wiggle-style cure to use in real life, what would it be?

AM: If there were a way to magically vacuum the word *like* out of people's mouths before they, like, use it, like, unnecessarily, that would be, like, great.

AP: This has to be my favorite question, ever. I obsess not only about what I like to call Piggle-Wiggle Parenting (how her cures play into real-life parenting), but also imagining funny imaginary cures for my kids' latest misbehaviors. These days it feels like everything has to happen *right now*. And, by the way, this is not just a kid problem; plenty of adults can barely handle a slow Internet connection without losing their cool. But for kids in particular this is a struggle since they've never known anything other than instant gratification.

My kids are astonished when I tell them about the "olden days" when we had to listen to the radio and hope the song we wanted to hear would come on, or if someone called and we didn't answer, they would have to keep calling back until we were home, or if we wanted to learn about a topic (and our family didn't have their own encyclopedia set), we had to go to the library and look it up using the Dewey Decimal System. So I love the idea of a cure for Impatient-itis, where everything in their world slows down and the world gets old-school; their cell phones dial like rotary phones, each text message takes a whole day to send, and selfies have to process for a week before they can see them.

Are you able to say what's next for Missy and her menagerie?

AM: In the second book, Missy cures whiny-whiners and smarty-pantsiness, as well as other habits, while continuing to make a life for herself in Little Spring Valley.

Originally published on Mental Floss (mentalfloss.com). Used with permission.

When a terrible storm blasts through Little Spring Valley, the upside-down house is in need of repair. But money's getting pretty tight for Missy. Will she able to get the money to repair her family's home?

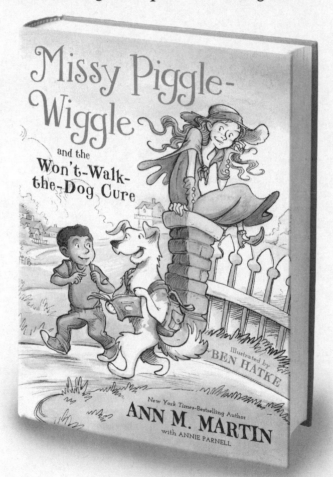

Keep reading for an excerpt.

The Storm

MELODY COULDN'T HELP herself. She let out a long scream. "AUGHHHHHH!" She screamed so loudly that she made herself cough.

Wag ran for a corner and stood facing it, his tail between his legs, while Lightfoot climbed all the way up Missy as if she were a tree and tried to burrow under her hat. Polite Lester, who could usually be counted on to remain calm, began to snort in a way that did not sound mannerly at all but was perfectly appropriate for a frightened pig.

Penelope, for once, had absolutely nothing to say.

"Is everyone—" Missy began to ask. But at that moment, thunder crashed again.

The attic was as dark as dark can be. *As dark as a pocket*, Mrs. Piggle-Wiggle would have said.

Missy held her hands in front of her face and couldn't see them.

"Where is everyone?" asked a tiny voice.

"Veronica?" said Missy. "Is that you? Are you all right? Let's all try to hold hands."

"I'm not holding hands with any girls," announced Linden.

Girls?! thought Tulip. *What about pigs?* But fortunately she didn't say that aloud.

What followed was a lot of scrambling around and cries of "Where's Honoriah?" and "That's my nose, not my hand!" and "Let go of my hair!" and "AUGHHHHHHHH!" (That was Melody again.) But at last everyone was holding hands and hoofs.

"Are we all okay?" asked Missy. She took roll call. She made sure she could feel Lightfoot on her head, Penelope on her shoulder, Wag's rump in the corner, and Lester's hoof in her left hand. Then she called out, "House? Are you okay, too?"

The house replied by opening and closing the door at the top of the stairs.

"Good," said Missy in her calmest voice. "This is a big storm, but we're all together and we're all fine. We'll just have to wait it out."

"We could pretend we're pioneers without electricity," suggested Petulance in a whisper.

"And we've been put in a dungeon," said Veronica.

"Who would put pioneers in a dungeon?" asked Rusty.

CRASH.

This time the clap of thunder was followed by a crash of a different kind. Missy heard something heavy fall above her. She heard wood splinter and glass break, and she knew that something very bad had happened.

She took roll call again. Four animals and seven children were accounted for.

"House?" said Missy. "House?" She paused. "Are you all right?"

She waited for the door to open or the stairs to creak, but there was nothing.

~~~~~

"I think the storm is letting up," said Rusty after a while. "It isn't raining so hard."

"The thunder is going away," said Melody, sounding relieved but not letting go of the hands she was holding, even though Rusty was trying to shake her loose.

Five minutes later, Missy looked up the stairs and saw a beam of light coming from the kitchen. "The electricity is back on," she said. "I think it's safe to leave the basement. But be careful."

Every single child in the basement ignored Missy's warning and went charging up the stairs like a bull. Tulip ran into Honoriah, and Linden tripped over Wag. They crowded into the kitchen and peered out the window.

"Ooh, look! Everything's all blown around," said Veronica with great excitement.

"The trash can is lying on its side," Rusty reported. "There's garbage all over the place."

"The farmyard looks like a lake," said Petulance. (That was a huge exaggeration.)

Missy picked up her phone. "Call your parents," she instructed the children. "Let them know you're okay."

"Trouble!" squawked Penelope from the front of the upside-down house. "Trouble!"

Missy hurried through the kitchen and the hallway and opened the door to the porch. She looked out into the yard, which was now dotted with holes full of muddy water. The golf ball floated in one of them.

Missy's gaze traveled to the right, and she let out a sigh.

"Oh, no," she said. "Poor House. Poor, poor House."

The very tall oak tree, the one Veronica had climbed earlier, had blown over, roots and all, and was leaning at an angle. Missy's gaze followed the trunk

up,

up,

up

to the top of the tree.

It had smashed through the upside-down house. The windows of the attic (or the basement, or the basement-attic) were shattered, and Missy saw glass glinting on the ground below. The roof and one of the third-story walls had splintered and caved in. Below, on the second floor, Mrs. Piggle-Wiggle's bedroom window was broken and another part of the wall had been smashed in.

"Poor House," Missy said again, and tutted just like her great-aunt would have done.

But then she straightened her back, told herself to buck up, and returned to the kitchen. "Make sure you keep your shoes on," she said to the children. "There's broken glass outside. I'll wait with you until your parents pick you up."

～～～